QUERENCIA

WINTER 2025

Querencia Press – Chicago Il

QUERENCIA PRESS
© Copyright 2025

All Rights Reserved

ISBN

978 1 963943 38 2

www.querenciapress.com

First Published in 2025

Querencia Press, LLC
Chicago IL

Printed & Bound in the United States of America

CONTENTS

POETRY

END TIMES

> green hum yellow hum red hum screech.
every night, crickets harmonize with the hum of changing lights. outside
the window, condensation hides my fear and muffles my prayers. streets
have laid empty night after night. not a soul graces the sidewalk below.
but i am here.
> green hum yellow hum red hum screech.
etching another tally in the crumbling brick wall beside me. the ninety-
fifth day has come and gone. i haven't slept once since the trumpet
sound. the sun is down to only a sliver of light every twelve hours. i
haven't seen the moon since day thirty-three. no sense in going out again
to find you. i am still here.
> green hum yellow hum red hum screech.
echoing the sound of praise outside waiting for the phone to ring. lord
please call me back. the walls are closing in. some nights i hear the faint
whispers of my mind sneaking up behind me. i already tried to run away.
that first month alone was running from the whispers.
> green hum yellow hum red hum screech.
evening of the thirty-third day, i did it. found your book, opened it, and
watched myself get swallowed by the hesitancy that keeps me here. i
know i should believe it, but every time i start over, nostalgia grips my
neck, curiosities squeezed out.
> green hum yellow hum red hum screech.
god! why is it so hard to get back to you? how many more days shall i
spend here pondering? for sixty-two days i have haunted these halls.
searching for the goodness of you in every vessel. squinting i stare into
myself,
> green hum yellow hum red hum screech,
>> and wonder if i'm the vessel.

—T Cruz (they/she)

HOW TO DROWN YOUR GOD
—after "333" by Jannat Alam

I.   make them tea. make it hot. scalding. volcanic.
tell them you added an ice cube. you lie. watch
them bubble and boil to the bottom & once the
liquid cools read them their leaves. divination.

II.   divination. pull out the bones. the stones. the
tarot. every card you pull is the five of cups.
tell them to stay away from the bodies of water.
they don't listen. they never listen. jump.

III.   jump. tie a rope to your god. plunge. down
into the darkness & the cold. tell them it's okay
to breathe in. watch the lungs become sorry they
listened. you lie & you lie & you lie & you lie.

— GABRIEL NOEL (he/they)

1

---

[1] the straightness of arrows. their lack of queer. stick figure anatomy, my center, a gnarled tendril. intercut with missing winter, its want for warm. intercut with consumption, pork. swords between toes, martyrs because two people can't exist with the same name. we do, somewhere. male genitalia held aloft: windchimes. every gun is smoking before & after the third act, my adopted mother exclaims onlyness, as in character death, ghost flowers at graves we don't share blood types with. no, you're not bipolar. but at least you are alive. what walt whitman said. that i have died so many times & have not yet lived. i am fruitless, haven't eaten fruit in weeks, i will not bear children nor will they one day bear me. the bloated gas can, four months of summer deep, an object that remains without motion will remain without closing. he/his proverbs. refrain. ellipsis. miscellaneous tools who promote an opening. i stim for hours at work, hours while i sleep. the bentness of arrows, unknown variable of splinters. the body is the same way, the one that was found of mine, the one who was identified. blood stays hidden until dictated otherwise. dante traverses paradise & its half-siblings for this, so the more real brands of pain can idle, discontinued. it's like wanting there to be an end to poems. most faucets leak, most oceans wish they could feel it. my other mother once died, then died once more. the tears between pages, or at least what we wished was absence. something that makes sense to hold onto. i've never said enough.

THIS IS NOT ANOTHER LOVE POEM

This is red weaving violet into evergreen,
the catalyst, the,
glaciers slipping under the weight of themselves,
five moons—everlastingly blue.

This is a confession,
an idea of fear casting like iron,
love having no formative taste for comparison
other than my lack of wanting to overturn otherness,
instead to writhe below the hands of it.

This is fervor impersonating courage,
pearls in place of diamonds,
flaw being my reason to fall but
I bury it again.

—SELENE CERIDWEN LEE (she/her)

MY BODY IS INHABITED BY INSECTS.
"Does your mother know?" —Guts, Leith Ross

They have been with me since the sixth grade, when a boy in my class
kissed me behind the recycling bin. I let my eyes unfocus on the texture
of the rust on the crate, lips closed and body frozen. I can't remember
what they felt like the first time, the bugs. I do know that a rustle goes
through my lungs each time I see royal blue.

We kiss once. I am not sure I want to, but we are drunk and you tell me
how pretty I am, so I open my mouth to your tongue and your teeth. My
lips are cut up and bruised the next day. I feel a soft, quiet buzz
underneath my cheek where you kiss me goodbye the next morning. In
that moment, I think they are honeybees aching for a drop of your
sweetness. They leave me alone for the following weeks, mostly, but the
sound returns occasionally at night when I think about the taste of my
own blood transferring from your tongue to mine.

The next time we are drunk, you ask me to kiss you again. I am sprawled
on the hardwood of our friend's apartment, using the coolness of the
flooring to stay focused on your words. I feel a buzzing grow beneath my
thigh where your hand is inching toward as you speak, and I know that I
don't want to be touched. I tell you this. You stand over me, and you are
silent for so long I try to blink you away, thinking I've imagined you. You
are there every time my eyes open. Eventually, you nod to yourself, slow,
and move to the kitchen. We make eye contact as you take three shots
back to back, and my ears go fuzzy. All I hear are fruit flies, loud and
frantic between my ears until you turn the corner out of my sight.

Later, I find you crying in the bathroom. I can smell the vomit coming
from the tub you are draped over the side of. I still don't want to touch
you, but you look at me with wet eyes and the quietest greeting I've ever
heard you give, and I cave. I cradle you there on the bathroom floor. The
bugs hate it. They want to crawl out of my skin. I want to scratch at my
wrists until all of the insects can go free and fly into someone else's
mouth, but I am occupied with gently massaging your neck and running
my hands down your back. I notice that I can't feel your tears anymore as
you press further against me. You nuzzle into my neck, kiss it, and you
ignore the way my entire body twitches. Shudders. I think of deseeding

bell peppers and wonder if I could do the same to my wrists, if only to help you cope.

We kiss again. This time, I know I don't want to. My tongue touches the roof of my mouth, waiting to form around the word *no*, when I picture your reaction. The saliva pools heavy in my mouth as I think about each of your eyebrow hairs moving to frown. Chewing through your lip so hard it bleeds with tears in your eyes. I blink, and for a split second when my eyes are closed, I see a body with an open chest cavity, bugs frantically crawling inside. I cannot tell if they are trying to stay or flee. When I open my eyes, I say yes.

Each time you ask, I think of that night when I cradled you in the bathroom and say yes. There are times I don't even kiss you back, but you never seem to mind. The insects inside of me have never been so aggregated. They often sat in my stomach and the tops of my thighs, but since you, it has been changing. They have become restless. Tired. Angry. Each of them shift to new sections, my organs becoming homes for the groups of them.

I hide the beetles humming and vibrating loud underneath the palms of my hands by being louder, bigger, even when I wish to be quiet and sleep. I am afraid of what will happen if people hear them, see them crawling beneath layers of my skin and dirt. I wear gloves, and when they multiply and shift to the entirety of both arms, I wear long sleeves.

We make eye contact, and my chest creates swarms of dying moths covering my lungs in distress. I hate cigarettes, but I smoke them now, just to burn them away. If I think about kissing you for too long, I can feel pieces of their rotting wings in every inhale I take.

The fireflies that live in my skull have lights that are dim at best and maimed at worst. Their wings feel heavy in my head, like they're flying through a snowstorm with wind so forceful you can hear its whistle. They hide from even me, burrowing inside of memories they are sure I avoid. (I want them to be wrong. They never are.)

Each time you and I are alone, the praying mantis that lives in my stomach tries to crawl up my throat. I am afraid of what will happen if I open my mouth and let it roam free. I do not know if it is male or female. I do not know if it will eat my head or yours should it ever succeed in crawling through the small gaps in my teeth and prying open my jaw. Sometimes, when I am alone and convince myself that liking someone is just meant to feel like this, I let my mouth hang open, waiting for the praying mantis to wake up, hoping with everything in me that it is hungry.

—KJ MILLER (they/them)

THE DAY I FINALLY GRASP THE CONCEPT OF LOVING MYSELF WILL BE MY LAST

because like that, the old me
will be dead. fresh kill in the
forest, swan song still on my
breath. the act of self-love
having fallen on me like a knife,
cleaves me in half, severing
shadow and light. i will be
reborn as a gemini soul, carrying
within me both new moon and
full moon. twin halves of a
whole, resurrected as one.

i saw myself in a vision—moth
soft & white-winged, stepping
out of the womb. meanwhile
my former body lay six feet
under, decomposing in a tomb.
the message of this story is that
you can heal from self-inflicted
wounds. in my heart lies an
unhatched swan goddess. i
hope to meet her soon.

—KAITLYN SUN (she/her)

dear diary, i know spotted lanternflies are actually spotted but i have to wonder sometimes if it really refers to their corpses scattered across the pavement, little red bellies crushed flat under grey appaloosa wings. some people have said that the act of killing one is useless, but then i saw on twitter the other day that everyone putting their all into the destruction of this invasive force is really doing something—what to believe? dear diary, i always choose the collectivist approach because if a group of people with a just cause in common can't get something done, what am i even doing here?

—**nat raum** (they/them)

none of the old | gods will | be useful to
us | all the pluots have gone | ripe the first
bite is taken | for me | false

fruit of the bone | pillar dendritic to its
bending antagonist | we've separated | vitamin d
from the aggregate | viridios

& her spine | as stone exclaiming
with weeds | my pelvis had | a cist burial last
spring | at the physical therapist's

office | i wanted to | cry but my
co-pay | didn't trust me | drupe in my
splint where | my knee once

tethered to | yes | my muscles are that
of rinds | yes | i have picked these | feet up
as offerings for trial | to deities

who sought to create | lessons out of my
body | i gave the pit | in my appendix | to a dead
pagan in a | hospital monstera

flowerpot | i gave it | to them before i
could prove | i had strength | to sit up
straight | again | the myths between

medical records were | seeds for the
spreading | what even is it | to eat | a flesh that consumes
us back | in return |

bygone prayer | doesn't seem to cut | the dirt
from the soil | tilth in the nerves | tissue | there's something
worth harvesting | here | i wish

to know all about | this the unpicked
fruit | the will of tendons | just a taste of | fiber & sugar
if i know | what fulfillment is

i promise to forget | what pain is | again

—LIAM STRONG (they/them)

SANDSTONE SPINE, LIMESTONE LUNGS

mother earth did not form me properly. i am not flesh or bone nor
am i an aspen. my brain mimics mycelium but a bit more sturdy.
when i whittle away what's wearing my bones there is a canary where
my heart should be and as she chirps away she keeps time while i
excavate the mine in my skeleton.
sandstone spine, limestone lungs.
i grit my teeth and bear it, carve a little further. i am searching for clay, for
an absence of sensation
begging for softness and fluidity to fill its shape, searching for clay,
searching for clay,
but pull my fingers away covered in chalk.
what good is this mountain to me?
sandstone spine, limestone lungs.

—ICARUS GREY (they/them)

BOX IN AN EMPTY LOT

Our house is made of saltine crackers
When the oldest turn their backs to adjust the television antenna,
we scratch at the walls and pocket the crumbs
Baby Tommy sits at the center of a circular rug,
an empty space like a hollow ring around him
Tommy's eyes are bigger and bluer every day
Dark perfect pupils like a skipping stone, sets their blinking lakes

They're the kind of blue you could dream a coin into,
praying that the oldest would stop shaking
the wardrobe in their bedroom
Like a man's shoulders with no answers,
like a vending machine withholding its charms
The sounds protrude like an off balance drier
with ranting boots inside, marching through the floor

Mostly Tommy just sits on his slice of SPAM
and coos at the lanky scissors snipping by
Sometimes the scissors bend down and fill the whole frame
with shifting, singing, impossible illusions
Sometimes the ceiling shakes with their fracturing voices
and salt stings his oceany eyes

—JODHI MATHER-PIKE (he/him)

	anthem stand, betrayal; the skin of your lover's throat so close to the gun at his hip	first time you saw a bone fight to be loved outside the body		mr.red-white-&-blue hawaiian shirt, claims again what isn't his
that joke & your tranny ass laughed all the way home	*yes, sir/ma'am, my bolt cutters tattoo is because i worked construction. oh, you too?*		you on the bleachers, drenched with sky. the lightning eating & all that empty	accidental white t-shirt contest in which nipple piercings make an appearance
mutton busting, n. sheep run from under the children, mud-slick with terror	& ms. rodeo princess did her duty, wiped the face of the littlest boy; his daddy grinned big teeth	Q: what of the underbelly? A: what of it?		last year, they hosted pipeline fighters. (to wit: coalition is not a home)
flag that big, cover the whole damn world		& you'll leave out the part about the cigarette	midwest whiteness, call that shit hungry. call it thief. fist around what it can get	
which is louder: the cuffs or the beer in his voice?	if the second coming happened right now, you think the emcee would lick christ's toes	(in all honesty, the cheese curds were pretty good)		*mama, i think we need to learn to shoot*

—Em Roth (they/them)

ROOTED

They've laid our way in lessons, multifarious, in being hated.
Standing in the rubble of one nation, playing god,
roots creeping in at us from those mahogany rooms, crafting claims
to strip us bare. Here, we shrink, deflating on scattered straw.
We've wasted time and love on these figureheads, made an identity by
waving their flags into austere air that has ceased to blow.

Our sunken eyes say it: We have thrown so many stones that we're blinded just
in time for Earth's turn, and by design. The powerful already don brown, while
we're standing in the detritus, the blood of others.
If it doesn't affect us, we still lay the table on this foundation and feast;
We, the gluttons—at once cannibals and fatted lambs,
Bloated we stand, with soiled feet only a flood can clean.

Let's find something we can do while all this is being done to us.
For now, I conquer the floors—witchcraft on treated wood and linoleum.
Can we will away these years by wringing, by polishing, while pretending the
center can hold as the bottom drops out?

I promised myself I wouldn't write songs of an empire's end,
yet here we are, cleaning before the schism for our sanity,
finding the places too low for them to see,
too aloft for them to touch.

—MAGGIE MCCOMBS (she/her)

A COLLECTIVE ANGER

the rock of rage breaks upon that
which it crushes
. our mouths , slit wrist to armpit
, howl the hysterical hyperbole of our hearts
, & our clenched fists
, like a reckoning of expletives
!! our sacred , seething anger , as if our bodies
were lit fuses
, a confluence of match and gasoline
, & too many bullets
, that only breaks when it breaks you
. my sorrow learned to drowned its misery
in a mason jar
of methamphetamine moonshine mayhem
& madness
. i know just how that onion feel
all wrapped skin-tight
as mummified umbrage
awaiting release .

—henry 7. reneau, jr. (he/him)

STOP-START SELF-HARM SPIRAL / I THOUGHT I'D GROW OUT OF THIS

i have more scars on my wrist from cat scratches than from blades, i've always been too scared to cut too deep, aching inside and out, head throbbing like i've never drank water in my life, like all i do is stare at screens or something, heartburn in my brain, a cloudy foggy day within all i can consider is: i want to die, i should die, pick up the gun, pick up the knife, pull the trigger, plunge the blade—have you considered therapy? have you considered the world isn't as bad as you think it is? chemical imbalance or is it just all the evil bombarding me, unloveable, unknowable even, nobody loves me *really* nobody knows me *really*, they say they care but there's no true understanding, there's no such thing, i'm hopelessly on my own, floundering in the dark, i make the motions, i accept the well-wishes, but i don't believe in them, how could anyone mean it? i can't even have a panic attack because i clamp down so hard, legs shaking, breath uneven, even if nobody's in the room—stop cold turkey. all i want to do is cry but the tears don't come until they do and then it's a waterfall of course just once i'd like to be held and kissed without having to beg for it without being afraid of it without wondering if i'll ruin everything i have ever known and ever loved by being too *much*, you know i feel a lot, that's why i even bleed, that's why i even am, that's why i can't talk about it, i whisper things in the night, i curl up in a ball and i'm not even by myself and it hurts, i've spent my whole life being ignored, you know, i can count the number of times i have been swayed in a lap with a hand smoothing over my hair since i started forming memories on one goddamn hand,   deep breath   —   !
    swallow it all.
make a cut or two, ruby red and glistening   anyway, how are you?

—BLUE JAMES (they/them)

THUNDERSTORM; 3PM

Rain
drops   like bullets
on the gutter   runoff

Punctuate   time
almost   imperceptibly

Leave   no exit
                 wound

        for an hour
everything   is Yellow

Lightning
strikes   my eyes
                 in a full-throated laugh

                 on its own
late   arrival

i am soaking   save my dry Cigarette

whispering   itself upward
        in one unbroken song

a dance
        done   in Stillness

the Clouds   are breaking
just beyond   the wall

and I am   Becoming
more   than
                  I had ever Thought to be.

—RYAN J. SKARPHOL (he/him)

27

RIBS FORM BOTH TREBLE AND BASS CLEFS.

I want a lover that sings offkey in the shower
while another kindred microscopes my mind.
Is it too much that both speak formal scientific nomenclature
and I teach them the language of clouds,
the rolling thunder in veins—more than thorns,
more than ribcage arpeggio?
There is friendship in professionalism.
An understanding of less words,
a refrain from the wrong words,
the other, a touch, vine of notes around shoulders.
Both clefs document gentle protection.

—KIM MALINOWSKI (she/they)

CERULEAN

To back up into delirium
I deposit your remains into
a you-sized coffin, knowing
you'll fit, tying you shut with
cerulean blue lace, taking
what remains to sprinkle off
deadened cliff edges, pursing
my lips, conceal-carry your
hips near my waist, stomach
expanding / pulling you closer
to this infinite inside of me.
Divine serendipity, closing
my eyes around the
circumference of your
Nordic skull, large to
endure the blows of
my impatience, my
generosity the bubbles
in your pop, hand over
my blue / purple nails.
"It is approaching,"
you say, as if the
clouds spoke defiance,
but what I hear is
"It is fading,"
as if meaning was
as temporal as
a head cold, thick
like your bacteria-
laden mucus down
your sucrose lips.
Yes, we are all body
and paltry in the
scope of it all,
yet I would lay
in a steaming bed

of you as the cold
froze over just to
see if we'd bloom
months from now.

—**ROBYN HAGER** (she/her)

THE ALCOHOL NEVER LIES

alleyways to streets to homes to beds to floors where i am laid instead where
memories are made you said   the alcohol never lies
but i suspect that it omits or at least convinces you of things that no one ever said
or did lies never told lips never kissed   the alcohol never lies
cars to paths to gardens to grass to barbecues and sunglasses to memories and
photographs on mantlepieces in the past   the alcohol never lies
from town to home to fast asleep to summer suns setting deep to my own mother
calling me and raising us from our dreams   the alcohol never lies
but i confess i've had a drink and am confined by form and rhyming so i'm not sure
that i think   the alcohol never lies
it makes me want to tell the truth but does not let me know it   perhaps i do not
know if the alcohol ever lies

—JOSEPH BLYTHE (he/him)

THE COLD SUN

I was in Ohio on winter solstice,
the cold disguised itself as the sun,
Its rays felt like ice cubes rubbing my skin.

The tropical sun that I had known in Malawi,
thundered heat as it roamed in the blue.
At dawn, it was a huge, red, semi-circle in the East,
at high noon, it was like a swelled, sparkling, colorless sunflower
whose thin strands of flames spiraled from the ground into the sky,
and created a small ocean on asphalt like a looking glass
for the zenith of the sky to groom itself from.
At dusk, my tropical sun, was a raw half-egg yolk that swam
in the albumen of twilight whose beautiful brush of its rays
wiped off the sins it committed by its scorch in the day.

Their cold sun cast a dull glow that needled my dead and stiff knuckles
that forked out of the plaster of paris of warm clothing.
I felt the cold nail my ear to a breaking point,
my crusty lower lip was buttoned by a ridge of dry blood.

—PROPH DAUDA (he/him)

Children enter the hospital with whooping cough and the shakes. They enter with bulges under their skin. They enter with small animals where their teeth should be. Children enter the hospital normal in all respects but for recurring dreams.

The girl as ghost stands in a field. She dresses in her own skin.

The girl as ghost stands in a field delicate with orgasm ache. Her bones grow tinny.

The girl as ghost stands in a field and sings mercy. Her lungs fill with rhubarb.

The girl as ghost stands in a field and opens her mouth. Mashed cherries pour out and everywhere it rains bird bone.

The boy as ghost stands in a shop and thinks of knives.

He today thinks of a knife to pull ligament from joint, joint from bone.

He today thinks of a knife to cleave through gristle and scare teenagers.

He today thinks of a knife to peel back skin. This knife with a handle longer than blade is rarely used. His customers prefer their meat wet with juice. His customers prefer their skin.

He today thinks of the cutlet knife, the sharpener, and many others.

—DAVID GREENSPAN (he/him)

WHAT THE BOMBS EAT FOR BREAKFAST

as a child you'd bring orange hard candies
you stole from your diabetic mother for breakfast
& we'd take turns sucking on the thick skin, eroding it
to nothing, a kiss between us

       now you've run out of food, say the raid will end soon
       say it's okay, you've learned to stay away from windows
       when there's gunshots, a hard candy would be
       heaven sent gift

& i like to imagine you as a bomb in flight
       maybe from the air you're free
exploded onto a stack of pancakes, red bacon
your debris, drowned in syrup, coughed out
brown sugar, savored the taste

as a child I watched you struggle to open
a paper carton of orange juice, little nails
working themselves around the sealed opening to your
golden prize, paper flecks fell into the juice but we
still gulped it greedily

       now over facetime you bend down to pet a stray orange
       tabby and tell me if someone eats a stray bullet
       it's their fault for being in the path, if a parent can't afford
       to house another family above them to be flattened first, they
       didn't work hard enough, refugees have it coming

maybe the ground being a new gash everyday, & swallowing
someone whole has left you rattled, maybe you're just a vessel for hate
its poison passing through you from ear to tongue to air but not staying inside
maybe we never sucked hard enough to get through your thick candy skin

as a child at sleepovers you'd wake me accidentally in early morning sun, rays
cast over your thin form as you prayed, barely a wisp, the light would knock

you over & the rays tasted like golden fried eggs on our tongue & now I can only
pray the bombs aren't hungry, that you taste like sour hard candy
                & you're a tough shell to crack

god i just wish i could pick you like a precious seed
out from the rotten orange flesh of war
but would you even want to leave your home
and grow somewhere new, how unfair a thing, to ask a seed barely born

—MICHAEL NEUWIRTH (he/him)

THE NEW ALCHEMY

—after Helen Frankenthaler's Mountains and Sea (1952)

The mountains and seas
that steady my landscape
march out of little orange bottles
with tight white lids.

Rivers of doses.
Mountains of milligrams.

Bubble-gum pink and blue pools
for bells that shouldn't ring
and kites that shouldn't fly.

Navy basins to stable the swings.

Blood-pink cliffs to hold the waterfalls
and soak up the sun's heat.

White ocean foam to anchor
the horizon to my feet.

Everywhere else is grass,
its roots feeding
from the medicine
seeping in the soil.

—CASEY CATHERINE MOORE (she/her)

DON'T CRY

"Don't cry for me. Don't cry for me."
It's not Eva nor Madonna who says it.

> Who says it is a breath on glass, an ant
> crawling across a countertop, a cough in the night.

In the night, the beggar who comes to you with
this utterance is unable to approach your bedside.

> They're unable to approach because they see all the lines across
> your body that can break your limbs as easily as fluorescent lights.

Like fluorescent lights, they'll only be able to flicker on and off
at the same times each day until you learn to look away.

> You'll look away and find those fault lines on your skin.
> You'll work hard to scrub them off, then the silence will come.

The silence will come, but in some small clump of dust remains that voice:
"Don't cry for me. Don't cry for me."

ALEX CARRIGAN (he/him)

Act Two

Some curtain or other has fallen.
A list of contents remain with no desire to congeal,
scooped up in the pockets of a withered ferryman and kissed with lips too cracked
to taste anything but the need to swallow.

You will forget me.
I will forget to take a moment for the dahlias and recall the need come Thursday
when grief is already welded into the glass of a once respectable vase.
That is to say, no walls could hold me.

—SELENE CERIDWEN LEE (she/her)

At rehabs in Florida, they take you to the beach on Sundays

Dear one, I am sorry
for the stench of black tobacco
which I know would break you
out in hives, but

I met a man on house arrest
whose ankle monitor still speaks to him
a thousand miles from home
and I have yet to hear from you.

Do you know, love,
why the moon never sets this far south,
or how the day turns slowly, not a flash
in the pan handle

instead the ocean imparting
a new shade over my eyes—

the incessant exhale of a rolling tide
receding, in dissipation approaching some permanence
like memory under layers of fresco
cerulean clouds.

I have never seen your Spanish sea
but I withstood a heart beating
against both coasts of a great continent

and if you were here,
there would be nothing left
for me to do but point
my finger at the moon for you

to see me once more within my quiet
desperate gesture.

I cannot tell you the truth
of what I've found,
but I want you to know
that I thought of you today.

—Ryan J. Skarphol (he/him)

EMPTY STOMACH, EMPTY HEART,
—For May.

You are more than your hunger, werewolf. You are more than the sum of
your claws and fangs and taste for mortal flesh. The equation does not
have to end in death. Your fur can bear wind not blood. Your mouth can
kiss instead of kill. Paws on earth, and ears full of song. Raise a howl,
raise a howl—!   Oh, werewolf, raise a howl, not for the hunt of meat to
tear into, but of love to sink into. You are not a killer, but a *survivor.* You
are wild and free and—   Loved!

—BLUE JAMES (they/them)

MOTH

Excerpts from a luna moth's diary...
[a broken human translation for better understanding]

click...| click...| click...| click...| click...| click...
midnight air / is it your {lingering} incense?
my {stretched} silk dripping darkness __________
i believe / o moon / look at i
{dressed} as your faintest bloom
incoherent, is i / excuse / for i
not the {kind} to have a voice / of my own
atremble, my shimmering gown, in {silver} trails
i, the phantom / flaunting moon's eerie glow
my {birthright}__________
i'm way past, the covert haunts
this {ghost} town has its own secrets
bizarre beauty / they say / wish i
had the {guts} to / dispute that
birthed in darkness, was i / hear the flame cry,
"fly / to me / my {alien} queen __________
your curved hind, i beg, bring your ecstasy sways"
swoon, is i / think, i not / o moon
hear me plea, as {cohesive} as i be
let me / my kin / let our eulogy be this ____________
once bound/ twice / doomed by {desire}
fire, devour, watch who {burns} the brightest^
~ flutter ~ flutter ~ flutter ~ flutter ~ flutter ~

{ } : *nearly lost in translation*

—ARANI ACHARJEE (she/her)

JOURNEY

It's not that simple. There are harbingers,
and so forth. The birds full throated
in their plunge, the sticky spill of entrails.
But what did we want, back at the start? To not be

trapped inside it. So the sky put forth its proposition,
and we burrowed from the place we were
to somewhere new: the same place, after all,
a ragged symphony of rain and creatures

calling in the dark, insolently nameless. A long time
journeying to somewhere; still the flesh follows.
We all make our choices, but if life
would let me write the next few lines, if I couldn't see

what's peering through the grass, always slightly
closer than you think. Each mouth is open,
toothless, plummeting. Sooner or later,
all of this will end. Probably

sooner.

—RIAM GRISWOLD (they/them)

THIS BODY HAS NEVER BEEN MINE

I make room for words—a hot mouth,
unwise to these own half moons, the arc of this well splitting.
I know I am a pit to suck on,
a hole to fill but not to reap with.

I could be happy being a wide, open river,
a wife if the water would have me,
a yew if wood could rhyme.

More of me in the comings that rise after the dirt lays than in this skin—
destined for pollen sooting lilies,
wet in winter's dew if it were gawkish and hid behind the grass,
the static that screams and hums and dances without limbs,
unceasingly soft, opinionated silence.

—SELENE CERIDWEN LEE (she/her)

　　　　—after *The Witcher 3: Wild Hunt*

dear diary, i don't know where the stories started but there is something about the lore of a plague maiden that is so delicious, so satisfying to imagine myself within—i'd even take the L and be a woman for just a moment if i could evaporate at will, split myself into four immaterial versions of the same wraith that surrounds an impending threat (a killer of specters) on all sides. maybe i am a monster, diary, but has anyone stopped to consider what made me this way? i have pins in every corner of my home—ties to something wicked that hold me here, in the world of the living, when i wish to depart in peace. what a relief it would be to feel these crooked skeletal fingers on my shoulder and snap my head around, jaw unhinged, and devour.

　　　　　　　　　　　　　　　　　　　　　—nat raum (they/them)

IN MY DREAMS, I WATCH MYSELF DIE. /heartfire. the dawn is singing and i am / learning to boil dissonance in my blood / each breath a refusal to harmonize. / *have you ever thought about it?* / the moon questions me. / in my dreams, i've woven a noose out of my own veins / i am hiding from the sea and / her quiet hands. / eyes ephemeral. i pretend not to see them. / in my dreams, i let my skin split open and find golden ichor / the taste sweet and floral. with it i swallow songs and stomach stars. / flowers sprout in my lungs / in my dreams, i watch myself die.

—ICARUS GREY (they/them)

SHOCK FRONT

i have always been at odds with the body,
how i own, comfort, resent one. a study calls
ours festivals, hidden below the murky

waters of our vision. we are unable to see
these bouquets of blinking light the same
way a reflection is unable to condemn

its own shape. at eight i begin to believe
in magic again, real magic like blushing cheeks
& shooting stars. i watch a fingernail regrow

itself after falling to the floor & witness bone
tucking itself back into bed. i knew i'd never
own a home without carpet or closets or winters:

my mother & i with our god-to-adam fingertips
defying daylight with an arctic crack–light
in the air between us. these moments, static

the way sheets are in sleep: pillow-clung
with sweat. how waking up drenched before
the sun means my brain beat a star in some

kind of race. dust sutures the universe
like a womb & creates white noise as a man
i love asks me to stand on his back until it

hurts. this stagnant design lingers in my mouth
like a pillar of salt & its cavity of stars. the light
left behind, its recycled visage.

—AMANDA NICOLE CORBIN (she/they)

BLOW YOUR HOUSE DOWN

Familiar,

     insidious.

Safe yet

     fatal still.

Flaws that neither of us count

     etched into our hands.

Emergency and crisis plans.

One hits the alarm,

     Our palms grip

too tightly,

     and

     love disguises harm.

Drag

     each other

down

the

steps.

Choking on the smoke,

Smooth-

     with smog and lies,

Detected in our throats.

I own yours,

     (you own mine)

Closing on the charred remains,

of what was once

      divine.

Hell hath no fury

of our own.

      My eyes

audacity to roan.

Comparison brought me here.

      (sulking in this ditch)

But should our house

crumble

down,

with three small pigs

      standing round,

A

   snarling,

     growling,

       big

         bad

           wolf.

Would they know

     who was which?

—SYLVIA MARIE (she/her)

My Mother's Sorrow

I carry my mother's sorrow. My father's, too.
The only difference is the weight
and where it lays to rest in my being.
My father caused my mother's sorrow,
and his mother dealt his out in tablespoons over years.
My mother's, in my heart.
My father's, on my tongue.

And I carry my own. Every version of myself.
Every year I have known, a new misery finds home in my skin.
I carry every hell I've walked through, every tear bled through
blood, sweat, and fear.

Sorrow is not just surface level, but bone deep.
Living in marrow that no longer serves its purpose.
Nothing but the suffering keeps me alive.

—MAY GARNER (she/her)

白 Snow

血 I lived in a state of rain.
公 I was hollow as the sail

主 stranded in the trees
非 by our tar-dark house,

吾 a monument for children
身 who wanted to drown

灰 themselves in the needles
头 of the shaking firs

土 before they came home
脸 to the serrated fire.

阅 I played alone.
黄 I ran my hands along

本 the blades of leaves
乌 and the trails of slugs,

发 cooked with cattails
无 in a witch's stump,

法 said there were fairies
遮 in the gut of every bud.

黑 I sang to the birds.
眼 I slept with the mice.

白 I was pale and starved
雪 as a familiar with

公 no master.
主 I was an unnamed child.

乃 I ate five apples
本 and choked the sink

身 with chunks of flesh.
很 I ate the heart of my

久 dear mother.
以 I slept in a glass vase.

前 I was silk as a rose.
我 I was red as ebony.

是 I looked into my mirror
人 and said, "Open sesame."

Translation:

白血公主非吾身，
灰头土脸阅黄本。
乌发无法遮黎眸，
白雪公主乃本身。
很久以前我是人。

Snow White is not me,
for with a head of ashes and a face of dirt,
I read a yellow book.
Black hair cannot shield black eyes;
Snow White is herself.
Once upon a time, I was human.

—CELA XIE (he/him)

Wide-eyed, wide mind, outstretched limbs, and toothy smile. Bouncing on one spot, Florence-forget-me-knot, clumsy, clutsy, and ditzy too, falling for the fun of it, back when adults didn't spit, glare, and snarl at you. Best friends with the sunshine and enemies with boredom, fidgeting, and dreaming were just the same you told them, and teachers tried to slow your pace with every so-called intervention but darling, how you spun and soared, outstretched arms and armour and all, never afraid for the tumble and fall, no cure and no prevention.

Sloppy cursive, collections they mocked, and every single snail saved, the frogs on the playground, the spiders in trees spoke a secret language you didn't have to read, see books smothered you gently and rocked you straight to sleep and characters were kind when the others didn't care so who could blame you when their worlds you shared, who could blame you when you just weren't there?

Hiding in the bushes for every show and tell, granted you had wishes and dreams and stories swelled-in that small brain they all tried to train but now you can hardly remember their names or the rules you memorised for each school day; did they win? Did they get you? Like the shadows under your bed, did they win? Now, you stand here with sense and semblance instead.

The memories come back now, two by two each animal speaks and tells you just all you forgot when growing up elite, gifted child syndrome meant you couldn't wince or bleed. Now crumbling as an adult somehow feels like sipping tea and knowing you can take your time, and everything will still be fine. I'm trying to find a way back to me. I left her locked in a blank white room, I let the others bully and tear, I was scared, but there's no excuse there; I hope she still feels safe enough to crawl into my arms, I'll crown a daisy chain, and we will laugh, dance, sing, scream, shout and holler, who cares if that's not lady-like, who gives a single bother, funny how one word unlocks all that you smothered.

Wide-eyed, wide mind, outstretched limbs, and a toothy smile. Bouncing on
one spot, Florence- forget-me-not, clumsy, clutsy, ditzy too, falling for the
fun of it, back when I didn't give a shit for the whispers and rumours; stares
and truth, adult truth, I should have severed every single word they
tethered...to you.

I'm sorry, little one, I'm sorry that I forgot how to jump and spin and fun-was
fed to me on a picket line of gadgets and gizmos a plenty, so I lost sight of
the wires flashing in our head, the urge to create and spill and make a mess
instead. The memories return now, injustice bares her head...but I can get us
both out. I promise we'll get through-
being the brunt of all the jokes, the clown, always misspoken, a lonely witch
drinking her potions...

It was never *you* that was broken.

—SYLVIA MARIE (she/her)

THE FIRST DAY IN SNOW

All my childhood, in my hometown of Zomba,
I had seen the angelic salt on only TVs and in books.
Then, in Ohio, wrapped like a burrito,
the lint of snow drizzled from the heavens
not like Zomba's hailstones that pelted us
as we danced and sang, in the huge but scattered
drops of November rain.

Swirling snowflakes carpeted the lawn white,
not like the Mwera and Chiperoni winds that left
us homeless as they raffled grass thatch and iron sheets,
shuffled silts and sand grains that dug and turned our eyes red.
It was as if a high rank of angels descended on downtown
Columbus curtaining it in a white veil.

—PROPH DAUDA (he/him)

Tacet

I will take:

Instruments

      out of tune,

Ticking clocks askew,

      The absence,   for which you   asked me

Not to leave you
      Over

We are not untied, not frayed

          Strings.

Chosen,
but without rings.

Clicking together lock and key
    in stolen moments.
    Fused,
    when we should not be.

Open,
Open;
Open:

Mouths, legs, arms,   you, me,   vast, wide, free.

What sounds, words, held in our throats, would rush?

We, we deafen
each other, by remaining

    hushed.

—CASEY CATHERINE MOORE (she/her)

LISTEN, WE DON'T SAY THAT HERE

—after daniel berrigan & danez smith

only *let us lose nothing* when this mouth was an edge
& you stepped back the length of the good sleep you
craved while the bombs, their obscenity, you said think
of the children & i did but all i could see was his
absence by which i mean the hole in his head when
they buried him, but even that wasn't sacred & you
want to stand around? here in the beast-belly i know
protest is performance or premature death depending
on impact, he chain-smoked until they shoved his
cheek into the ashes & i guess that's the middle
ground, the dirt, the half-view of the sky while you on
the sidewalk, the curb, the center never holds but
blames like the first fist thrown, the fist of a
man-thought-god & when you mistook the wagon for
an ambulance i remembered that hurt is a word some
people only read in poems *no poem to free you* but
the stones the child's wrist & flight &

—EM ROTH (they/them)

A LETTER TO THE LAST PERSON STANDING ON EARTH

Dear stranger,
long winter trails next to your empty tea cup.
a touch starved heart coils on the top of the hearth, the dying embers barely
scratch your soul. the moon peels your lips like juicy clementine and floods
your balcony in belated yearnings…

your sweater is a scandal of two yarns, housing your warm-blooded
tantrum at the cost of violated intimacy.
your bones are yet to see the lights but the music oh! the music that
survived the colossal history and ornate museums!
but you are to never haunt one.

winter is climbing on your vertebrae in serpent motion and it's okay if burnt
milk sticks to your burner like stained residue from last autumn.
it's okay if your eyes sing of the storm when you sip on the sun.
it's okay, really, to slip in a cacophony dream inside your back pocket.

this hushed planet is your graveyard—a solitude tranquilizer.
so let the frost pierce your skin,
let the ocean claim your veins,
let the soil bloom in marrow blossoms.

so sleep, dear stranger. sleep to dust.
you've been here for a moment, you've lived the last goodbye.
sleep tight, stranger.
rest easy now that it's blue and grey.

—ARANI ACHARJEE (she/her)

dear diary, any time i start up a new *pokémon x* save file, professor sycamore asks *a few quick questions* and one of them is *are you a boy or a girl* and i always feel personally attacked because buddy, that's not a quick answer. i've written before about standing at the intersection of two brands of indecision—agender, bisexual—but there's really more to it than a refusal to commit, which i'm still convinced does not live within me. i mean, look at me, diary—does the volume of the cry i choke out when someone else leaves me really say *commitment issues* to you? i beg for stability like something worse than desperate and find it eventually in my queerness. dear diary, i am a greedy bisexual, an apathetic agender, and i don't see the problem with it. my love for others is endless; my sense of gender is gone. and i am a pacifist—i shall let them be.

—**nat raum** (they/them)

seven times seventy times,
i prayed for healing,
through the bay window   at the front of the house.

carved my name in dust,
with my pointer,
on its sill

to the frame,
i traded my faith
                to live
manifestations in lieu of prayers
tears in lieu of worship
forgiveness, for myself,
      in lieu of repentance.

my cup overflows as it did before.
i still bear the cross!
      (in case i'm wrong)

      Perhaps I am.
maybe I should turn back,
      repent.
Bathe my eyes in
fractured sunlight,
      still kneeling,
wait for barren branches
      to take me
and for blossoms to
      bring me back.

      —T CRUZ (they/she)

[*TRIGGER WARNING*]

angry Black man is a trigger word in every government building. in the penitentiary, it is the way it has always been. if I write about what has been done to Black folks, by white folks, is a trigger warning to the editors of literary journals to claim solidarity with BIPOC writers, but wish me luck in placing my work elsewhere. trigger is the part of a gun that empowers white folks to decide when Black folks will die. *hey nigger!!* is the trigger word for every Negro's double-consciousness. is the trigger word for feets don't fail me now. is the trigger word to get all Stepin Fetchit saucer-eyed rabbit-in-the-headlights stereotypical. every Black child dead in the street is a trigger for police to act like they ain't the one who did it. Molotov cocktail is the trigger word for niggers only going to burn the wrong side of the tracks, is a trigger word for once the DOJ leaves it will be business as usual. justice under law & due process are trigger words for Black folk who are suffering from delusions of better than it used to be. blind bitch justice is white & racist, & not to be trusted. if I see that bitch caning her way down the street, I'm gonna push her mandatory minimum ass into traffic!! angry Black man is a trigger word on every daytime talk show, in every university classroom, at the Social Security office, is the trigger word for ban critical race theory, like it's something that hasn't been historically proven to have actually happened to us. knowing who We were, who We are, will trigger whom We come to be. trigger word is a warning to guilty cell-soldier racists who know Black folks ain't forgot shit. angry Black man is a trigger word for chickens come home to roost. Black Lives Matter is a trigger word for radical militant outside agitator, for Panthers packing gats in the Statehouse, is the trigger for Ronnie Raygun better pray his feets don't fail him now. *are guns in Black hands the trigger word for Black folks have a right to defend themselves?* what makes you think WeShallOvercome by lawyering with their laws, praying to their God, non-violent protesting by permit, or waiting for due process will set us free? trigger warning is July 1919 in Chicago, the Tulsa Massacre, the Rosewood Massacre. Is Trayvon, the Rev. Dr. MLK jr, Breonna, Michael, Tamir & every nigger lynched in the Red Summer of strange fruit. legal lynching is the trigger word for Black folk there's your fucking precedence—is the trigger warning for somebody, please, tell that nigga to get out the street. is the *content warning for explicit language & examples of violence.*

—henry 7. reneau, jr. (he/him)

WINNOWING

naturally, the chaff is harvested
like rubber from a cock.
i gave ten exes ten
ghosts. story problem:
how many lives am i
left with. we stim wood sealer
off one another, fireweed along
the edges. tanagers twill
italic, the butter loses
stature in the fridge
as the power runs
out, my father declares rom-coms,
not skin cancer, will kill
him. if there are history
books, i don't want to
be in them. a meaningless
meaningful life exists where
we fuck & no one is
compartmentalized into a bathroom
drawer. the story ends
simply with that—
ending, a method we're somewhat
very used to. i've scraped ice
off all their windshields. i've done
my part. if all my excess isn't causing
us trouble, then i'll continue
to tumble amaranth, russian thistle,
the detritus. not all garbage is worth
looking down upon.

—LIAM STRONG (they/them)

Night Vision

It's lost, he said.
You won't believe the eyes.
You mean my eyes?
No, the ones it watches with.
They're bright as flashlights,
burning through the dark.
And yet you say it's lost.

The moon made boot prints on his face,
trailed fingers through his hair.
Yes. I used to walk with it,
walls of glass to rivers,
the night a roof over our heads.
It swallowed us, but still I saw the stars.
And now?
Even the soil's stripped of quartz.

He said, *I printed posters.*
Dozens spitting from the box next to our bed.
No picture?
It doesn't photograph well. I described
the way it whimpers in its sleep,
the fleecy cradle slung from hip to rib
where it let me rest my head.
I pressed staples through the yielding flesh
of trees, left white shapes that fight against the wind.
Now rain has bled the ink.

We were standing by the river,
water licking at our feet.
What does it want?
You mean its function?
No. I want to know what *lost* is.
He said, *I miss the rustle*
of its breath across my cheek.
It would bound through mud, then dash
around my house, a thousand prints
across the floor and walls and ceiling.

And the eyes? *Well, I say eyes.*
How many teeth? What sounds
rumble from its throat? *I'm cold at night.*
You can't know the things I've done,
the food left on the stoop,
the moons I've howled at.

I put the shadows in my trunk
and brought them to the river.
Waist deep in the river,
I unfolded and unstitched them,
used their gauze to sieve for gold.
What did you find?
Nothing,
which in a way is something,
depending what you seek.

I found the edges of the infinite,
as I had nowhere else to look.

As the moon unspooled across his jaw,
I asked how it escaped.
Slowly, he said.
The scent of lilies at his throat.
His eyes a net
that let the stars fall through.

—RIAM GRISWOLD (they/them)

ARE YOU HAPPY?

I think I'm dying of loneliness.
That isn't a hyperbolic statement, I'm dying
of loneliness, didn't know that was a thing.
We are breakfast, lunch, and dinner.
We are the same meals like clockwork
our mouths eat the food without knowing sometimes.
You haven't called me *baby*
in an increment of time I can't measure.
12 months since we've had sex
empirical data we *can* measure.
Does a number matter? I was taught to
measure your life in love
and I believe that's mostly true
but time is measuring us
like rations on a plate
food we don't want.
It tastes so much better
when you really want it.
I mean *really* want it.

Went out on my walk and made myself sad.
I saw a couple in the distance, one
pulled the other in for a kiss
the kind where the kiss
is pulling them, new-ish love.
It wasn't that I didn't want them to have it.
I wanted to *want* that for us.
The desire is (eating me)
alive
I'm so fucking starved
to be that dinner staring back at a mouth
I want to be grabbed and growled by someone
like a meal that hasn't been eaten in years
like I'm the only thing they craved
before being ravaged
like nothing else has ever tasted better than me.

I think I'm dying of loneliness.

—ROBIN PERCYZ (she/her)

65

THE MAKING OF ANGELS

Did you change the shape of men's bodies
When you undressed at my eyeline
When my sisters' bodies, not even stretched in their first full yawn,
Needed to be told of their impulse to create desire
When my mother passed on your heritage
Fuck him whenever he wants, or you'll encourage wandering eyes,
wandering hands,
~ Another man of God gone haywire ~
And, listen dear,
It's all on your watch
Before those breasts fill the fabric
Before the first drip of stained blood trims those high white socks
Take it in
Do you understand desire my girl?
Okay, now put a lid on it.
Good.
Lower those eyes just a little.
There.
~ You're an angel my dear ~

—JODHI MATHER-PIKE (he/him)

ANTI-SONNET
    —after Arianna Monet

i'm recalling the scene in *Almost Famous* where Penny Lane gets her
stomach pumped & she is still fucking beloved, girlypop glory. she
experiences pain. it's [quick, nearly footnoted to] painless. no one knows
but in the [extended cut of the] film i fall in love with Penny while she
wanders Morocco because her body is PERFECT, but [not] in the way
people typically render perfection, because i [don't] actually love her for
her. it's easily unexplained. my parents [almost] named me William & no
one wanted that. let's be serious. my peripheral nervous system had a
birthday wish in the year 2000 that was [never] resolved. a couple
decades & change later, my liver pinches itself to keep awake, the
risperidone, lithobid, mint dissolve from the seroquel, latuda, purple-
yellow like unripe berries. [maybe] it is wrong of me to feel this way. she's
fictional, of course, but my somatic nerves tell the truth. my brainstem
often translates tripping into tripping, a collapse like origami into a
puddle as an overdose without friends to catch me. there will be a
cesspool drowning into the dirt next to my head [in this future], the one
where i hate [envy] Penny's [perennially able] body. [if] my pain has to
have a chronology, my arteries taut against a stumble, [then] allow me to
fall with grace, or [at least] something like it.

—LIAM STRONG (thcy/them)

WHERE NOW?

Here the wind angers the face of the clouds

     it crosses plains that have been nailed
          to the ground

        as their roots drip endlessly
       towards the root of the earth.

The light hits the north different

the sun lowers the horizon
and days turn into a liminal space

rays burn the trees under an orange dream
       that asphyxiates as months go by

The earth falls into winter
and the copper atmosphere
    doesn't fully manage to wake people up.

once more I stop recognizing the trees
and the branches where the void of the birds
shrinks the heart.

I am surrounded by a beauty I don't yet understand.

Or maybe
     I have traveled too far.

—CAROLINA BUCHELI PEÑAFIEL (she/her)

I'M NOT

a rag doll
to be reckoned with.
No accidental diva
in variations of viola

I don't simper
I simmer.

I believe that rest
is for the dead
but I'm tired,
rundown with each kick

I snarl but
lose a bit of fight.
I'm all checklist
and all scribble.

If I could shrink into nothing
I would have by now.
I puff up my chest
because I can only
get bigger, take up my space,
go at that fast pace

believe that there can be a winner.

—KIM MALINOWSKI (she/they)

i toss doodads and whatsits into my cart i go dewy-eyed at bright
knickknacks and i think *oh another cat tree!* another soft place for feline
paws to rest and nevermind they're perfectly fine with the cardboard
boxes their litter shows up in prints of dewdrop glittering forest nights
and moons dipping crystalline into riversides dopamine hits dumping 40
different pins and stickers into my cart and shuddering to imagine
clicking PURCHASE and not going into debt showering indie creators
with my money instead of veterinarian visits and sustenance a thousand
subscriptions to a thousand different little Patreon clubs drown in art
drown in cute little trinkets wash myself with candy striped scarves and
cook every meal in the prettiest little homespun pottery and drape
myself in a blanket formed by love and priced according to how much
sweat blood care was poured into it tender hands painting a canvas and
then hanging it on my wall for me to lick and drink every bit of noise
calorie heat i'll never need to sleep or sprinkle my tongue with generic
storebrand sugar again

—BLUE JAMES (they/them)

Abaxial Bends & Begonia Breaths

what am i if not petaled bones & frothy
algae foams. spidersilk webbing on my tongue,
catching mayflies & fowler toad songs, head
weeded out of fuzzing foxgloves & falcate crassulas

i am still carnivorous & barbed-mouthed,
puffy yarrow & marram grass sprouting
in head-hairs, a catch of begonia blooms
netted in my throat

breaths cobbled together
honeyed & nectared
not fully formed
not fully feathered,
still an abaxial bend away
from these ravenous roots

—Katrina Lemaire (she/her)

STAINS

S p i l l i n g

D
  r
  i
   p
    p
   i
    n
   g

Stains
I don't know
how to remove
Mami, what
gets blood out
of clothes?
I never learned
The way it sits—
    a wax sealed
    envelope,
    Mars of
    oxidized rust,
    a poppy atop
    a crib sheet
Settles
My hands
Steady
Maybe,
this too
is holiness—
    a pulsing clot,
    crimsoned string,
    a perfectly
    tidied womb

I learned
How free
Love
     f
       l
    o
 w
     s
Blued.

— LIZ MÁRQUEZ (she/her)

TODAY

Where yesterday's colors
blend in rainbows of gated breath,
and bird song blends
as figures of speech
dance the tango, figures of late
debate ground soil
and toil in imaginary states
of tomorrow. The city
of brotherly love, in its finest
cloth, greets.

I can. I will. I fly.

Wings wide,

I wonder—

do homonyms   do strong verbs
ever crave   tire
originality   easily

does ground soil   do (ch)urns
ever desire   wish for
(f)light   another turn around the sun

are feathers   do seeds
curious about plants   desire (f)light

do dark edges   do picked pockets
ever crave light   envy suspender pants

what might Amelia   does a love for a city
Bedelia say to Amelia   know eternity
Earhart if their flights
crossed paths come night   Today. Can I. Will I.

Fly.

—JEN SCHNEIDER (she/her)

MY THERAPIST TOLD ME *YOU DON'T NEED TO ATTEND A CHURCH THAT DOESN'T LOVE YOU,* AND YEARS LATER

I remember the pastor at Parkland Immanuel who spoke in tongues.

I remember the choir director at Second Liberty who spoke in tongues.

I remember my mother spoke in tongues once.

        When was the last time I spoke in tongues in a church?

I speak in tongues before I enter a theater.

I speak in tongues before I enter a school.

I speak in tongues before I enter a prison.

        When was the last time I spoke in tongues in a church?

I speak in tongues when I'm driving.

I speak in tongues when I'm making love to my future spouse.

I speak in tongues when I hear my two year old nephew's laughter.

        When was the last time I spoke in tongues in a church?

I speak in tongues when I wash my hair.

I speak in tongues when I comb my hair.

I speak in tongues when I scrunch my hair.

        When was the last time I spoke in tongues in a church?

— MAYA WILLIAMS (ey/they/she)

MEET ME AT THE CANDELABRA TREE

You nuzzled in my hair, *I'd go anywhere—*
And we'd meet and you'd tell me about how a baby's intestines first start
outside of its belly,
Then tuck back in, as if teaching her how to constrict.
To bend, to brace for fear, then feel
Calm, again.

Manic, prismatic colored sunsets make my bump
— Where you're found —
An almost sea-siren red. I cup my hands around the belly, *thump,*
Just there. Breathe life into her, if we dare.

Every day, saying what she might like to do someday:
Nestle treetrunks that have seen decades of tears;
Meet under pine cones and trestles that block out the sun—that feeling of being
buried under earth, that tells us what's important (to stop doing
What We're Supposed To Do).

S'mores that are topped with strawberries,
Slathered with the promise of peanut butter, or wrapped around your
best friend's arms
As you light the fire. Add a little bit of kindling to meet the stars,
One more time.

Dexterity in love is wanting
To hurry the moment where your eyes meet mine, to show you how a
candelabra tree
Favors flight—
While at the very same time, placing my arms around myself, keeping
You wrapped—barley and twine—
Around me.

Pregnancy and trees,
Swing me, swing me.
Both wrap; both give in,
Willingly.

— LESLIE CAIRNS (she/her)

76

Wild Greens Soup
1930's Appalachia

Fingers of frost stretch across the windows.
Seasoned wood crackles in the wood stove
while I stir the last salty pork knuckle
with a handful of beans, wild greens

into a pot of well water just off the boil.
Each stir is more a wish as the day considers
getting warm, sweet herbs summon cravings.
Fall's harvest now a collection of empty jars.

The cupboard's breath dust and dead moths.
Morning casts its pink sap over frost-risen clay
as I shepherd this thinly feathered brood
towards the cotton-strewn spinning room.

Today we will piece broken strings, weave
cotton scraps to make them something whole.

—Kimberly J Simms (she/her)

GROUNDED FLIGHTS

on a chittagong rooftop beneath heat clogged skies,
I lay with my *nannu* on beach chairs, gazing
up at airplanes. the plate of cactus-cut
fries balanced on my belly a soother
for my discontent in your absence.

in our hushed, potted guava cocoon,
I unearthed my secret grievances:
I enjoy nothing when dad isn't home. nothing.
training on the other side of the
planet, I imagined you having fun without me,
riding merry-go-rounds and teacups,
throwing pounds of pennies into wishing wells,
making sundaes, seeing elephants at the zoo,
and telling someone else the tale
of a thousand thieves.

I did not understand your ambition—
the turning of pistons, goliath machines,
math problems the length of my arms—
how much this calling defined you.
on our walks through kirkland park, in toronto,
to distract me from the geese, you would point up
at a plane and say, *let's measure the distance
and angle between us and that little flier up there.*
I felt the oceans between keenly during your trips,
dreamt of you soaring over pacific waters, above
the cloud line, and still the fish were large enough
to snap at the wings. octopi tentacles snaked
around the plane's body, tugging it toward the
deep and squid released ink to make the pilot go
blind. I made mum phone you in the morning,

waking you from your jetlagged sleep, to hear
your voice. laughing, you reminded me that fish
can't reach planes. *what about blue whales?* I asked.

you chuckled; said you bought me sneakers that glow
in the dark, joked you would take me to the aquarium
after you flew back home.

now you grow vegetables in the backyard:
flowering purple cabbage, rigid celery stalks,
onions, speckled squash, striped zucchini—your
green fingers till the soil with mechanic precision.
for the past five years, you've sat on the old brown
couch in pursuit again, but with little luck, awe turned
to nightmare tentacles threading through you,
keeping you earthbound.

I feel the distance keenly, again;
no math problem enough to calculate
the depth of hurt, the fissures in your body from
years of the industry fracking you, your willingness
and wonder. airplanes are now the stuff of static life—
the trips not taken, the vacations missed, the visits
to grandparents made too late, and the need to
say no because there isn't enough...

still, sometimes you pause, look up at the sky and smile.
you ask, *can you measure the distance between you and the plane?*

—TANISHA E. KHAN (she/her)

LOST GEOMETRY

It's more than a glitch in the matrix—
it's a cataract spread wide
in the eye of the mirror,
leaves folding like dead hands
to the ground's thrum.
Toes in the static, tanning
on the backs of some unborn coast,
luminescence burned out before it began.
Cloves turning purple for a second,
just long enough to taste the strange geometry
of time bending sideways.
Clouds know this—
they've eaten it,
drunk it down in fistfuls,
spilled their secrets on the broken pavement.
Man and woman,
they've seen it, too—
the weight of things unseen,
the hollow ache under the skin
where what is concealed grows sweetest.
Call my name into the pit,
see how it echoes back like a lie half-spoken.
I was salt,
tailored for the insult before I could even feel
the weight of my own skin.
I was the fish with no mouth,
the silent part of the ocean,
hooked in the Mediterranean's raw throat.
The sun? A serpent that twisted its tongue
into the shape of a promise,
flayed the kite and watched it burn.
I know why they whisper,
that ancient murmur thick with the dead,
a Norse dialect choked on forgetting.
Blurred,
fractured into shapes we dare not call names.

—RACHEL CHITOFU (she/her)

INTERNET LOVESONG

i made a playlist today, and after you
that somehow feels like an achievement: picture the
glow of the mosh pit and a thousand anthems you ignored
what can i do to avoid the glittering synths that you
blasted at 1am to piss me off? always so polished
and fragile—i was only ever afraid to drop you
is it possible to be gay without crippling anxiety?

i doomscrolled today, and next to thinkpieces
about the supposed ethics of ecocidal
straightness, all i could see were your portraits
of an ideal—the brushstrokes you measured out
in cornflower-blue lines, straight like the girl
i would have been. your scribbles announcing everything
i never was to you—too liminal, too much—your graphite
like a digital poison. can you generate me with chatgpt
make me your picture of AI fuzz, unrealistic details
yet if you back away, do i look like a person?

—mk zariel (it/its)

in my throat   the words i can't speak   tie
themselves around my bones

my anger is old
          it has brought down mountains
                              thrown stones
                                    closed abysses
for millions of years
i've felt my anger uproot the earth
serrating plains   and turning pinnacles   to sand

there is no relief in a familiar face   no comfort
in memory
no life after death   no god watching from above
below   no one punishing

once I was a hardly noticeable crack in the ground
                    until i was ruptured by words

—CAROLINA BUCHELI PEÑAFIEL (she/her)

APPLES

Hello Kitty is five apples tall.
Depending on the variety I'm fourteen.
They never clarified how round Hello Kitty was.
The magazines growing up let me know I was round.

Diagrams helped point out my distinctive apple type.
Not the ideal hourglass
or a juicy curvy pear.
Just a squat apple on the counter was how I looked.

I saw these evaluations and took them on board.

I thought you could lose ten pounds in a month because Women's
Health said so.

You don't see that now though.
One should only lose two pounds a week now.
No month is five weeks long.
Some are,
but not thirty-five days.

So,
it doesn't count.

I knew at minimum you should always be able to see your feet.

Unless your boobs
and only your boobs,
blocked the way.
And even then you could be fat.

Those body type diagrams never showed a size 00.
Everything else visual did though.
Just to clarify for me,
what wasn't said aloud.

—MEGHAN ALBIZO (she/her)
First published by Audi Locus

THAT I MIGHT BE HOLY IF TO BE HOLY IS TO LOVE

That church on Vanderbilt stares at me like love is real
and it's evident in my camera roll.
I've taken countless photos of its strong lines
tall peaks like daggers stabbing the heart
of the sky.
My eyes are fixed
like it's the most beautiful person in the world
promising to stay.
Orange and red leaves have kissed its stained glass windows
through the fall
leapt
from the trees
in the way
people leave.
Absence is a prayer that you're true
while standing in life's gray house
of loneliness.
I take its photo like I'm seeing it for the first time each time
each click a kiss on its forehead
and surely the neighbors think I'm strange
some sort of crazed lover with my camera in its face
to make sure it never goes away
at least from the palm of my hand.
I always find a new way to see this church
in its changing body
covered in shadows and still it's so bright
when I stare into its soul.
It makes me almost believe love is real
even when its insides are not where my hands or heart can ever go.
Even when the world's inevitable mind longs for something new
it makes me almost believe
I can be a church for someone to love
a church someone can enter and stay.

—ROBIN PERCYZ (she/her)

One More Hope to Nourish

How sweet,
    of the moonlight glistening across
    my window as Dinah's voice
    tendered a melody strong enough
    to undo my worries of tomorrow.
How vexed,
    of my body turning this way and
    that—my mind unsure if this
    peace could last always. My
    strength is like dust to the wind.
    I drown my tears in the privacy of the night—
    believing Dinah's call that a rainbow will be
    before me, that my yesterday was blue, but
    tomorrow doesn't have to be, too. I drown
    my tears in the privacy of the night—
    praying that when morning comes, my
    mind will also remember its light.
How magical,
    of daybreak to return to me once more—
    brushing its patterns across my window
    slowly enough to make a royal entrance,
    but quickly enough to teach me to let go.

—Tony Nicholas Clark (he/him)

PEDAGOGIES OF VIOLENCE

today i looked at the dead child on my phone
and wondered how many of my students
would've killed him. teaching in the heart
of the empire and on good days we make

cannon fodder. most days we teach them
hurt and pretend it is something other than
the american tradition. i know, i know: this
is not any way to think about the young,

this is not any way to think about the future,
ill-gotten as it is. each child is precious
but, today, what can i hold that is anything
other than bloodstained? these small hands

in mine, and i am staring at the eyes of those
come smiling to our door, simpering violent
little nothings to hungry ears, as bullet-hearted
children stumble towards their promise.

—EM ROTH (they/them)

a girl created by working hands, love and trauma (in every magnitude), and
blood from three beautiful cultures—
"shouldn't you teach her spanish?"
"where's the feather in her hair?"
"why isn't she dancing the hula?"

—

i stare back at my reflection,
eyeing the precise features The Creator and my ancestors decided to give
me:
the little slant in my eyes that arrives when I smile, the feature
other kids would poke fun at growing up—*how are you a Mexican
with small eyes?*
the polynesian body, the thick bones that prepare me for a battle
that may come one day, when we reclaim the land that is rightfully
ours—*the island of polynesia*
the bump on top of my "Indian" nose, the bump my glasses
conceal—*I touch it in the mirror, smiling and frowning.*

—

the fingers of my ancestors applied these features on me during my
creation,
because they did not see me as *half* or incomplete;
i was one of them.

—

assimilation is a deliberate evil,
the colonizer sung the lullaby to his Mexican, Polynesian, and American
Indian subjects, draining the culture from beaten, dead, and haunted bodies,
swearing that the savage in them will be erased, saving the white,
enterprising future.

—

i grew up assimilated from ⅔ of my creators,
and the incompletion was evident—the jarring nature of my existence
burdening my life. i was living off of the tombstones of my ancestors—
everything they had fought for was disappearing in the blink of an eye. the
colonizer wand that waved the spell, *"FORGET THEM"*, was working.

—

i woke up one morning and greeted the sunshine,
it conveyed words to me without saying anything—*a message from mother
nature, dear girl. never forget your people.*

i pondered about the meaning, until it came fast—
an illumination blossomed on the *ofrenda.*
then, while i was walking outside, i found a feather.
shortly after, i found an old picture in my memory box: a photograph of me
dancing the *hula* as a small, baby child. my belly protruded from the skirt.
the message was clear.

i danced across the trail of truth and glided across the river,
until i entered the land of liberation and saw the hands of my people,
extended. i reached for them, accepted, and was brought to the refuge of
my identity. there were *hammocks, tipis, hale nohos, and wharepunis* and
food and people—
music graced the place, blends of instruments and voices swimming
between my ears. each person looked at me.

  "eres una de nosotras."
  "kākou."
  "kei a tātou koe."
  "lomasumi'nangwtukwsiwmani."
i nodded, then cried.
  because though i come from three beautiful people,
  i am ultimately still one person—a blend,
  in this
  (*vida loca 'ōpulepule ola — tauoranga whakawehi   koyaanisqatsi*)
CRAZY LIFE.

         —M.S. BLUES (she/her)

WHAT I KEEP

I keep the quiet things—
the scrape of the chair across the kitchen tile,
the way sunlight pools in forgotten corners
at 3:47 p.m. in mid-September.
The September you stopped calling.

I keep the echo of my name
said by a voice who no longer calls,
your heartbeat fossilized in the hollow of my chest.
I keep the scent of the sea
that clung to my hair one summer spent in your grasp,
salt pressed into the waves
as if it, too, knew how to hold on.
If only the ocean could teach you how to stay.

I keep the ache of wanting,
the kind that turns ribs to rust,
each breath scraping against the memory
of something I almost had.
Something you never fought for.

I keep myself in pieces,
pressed between the pages of books
I'll never finish.

Each word a bandage,
each story a promise
that one day I'll learn
to keep *nothing* at all.

      —   Not even the memory of your touch.

—**MAY GARNER** (she/her)

Is she the next Britney Spears? Could there be another Britney Spears? Has anyone ever kissed like we did at that bar sober in the middle of the day? Britney is a once in a generation kind of talent, her star power unparalleled, her stage presence so magnetic—that's what all the fans type furiously and post online. They type, in all caps, that "Toxic" came out when Britney was just twenty one. In that video: Britney as femme- fatale, Britney as cunty flight attendant, Britney wearing nothing but a skin colored thong and crystals—not rhinestones—individually glued to her body. Almost nude, glinting. My 85-year-old aunt recently asked me what the difference between a rhinestone and a sequin was and I said a rhinestone is a prism, more of a jewel, and she said so a rhinestone is fancier? and I said I guess— but both a rhinestone and a sequin pale next to a crystal. At twenty one, I was sloppy, my days blurry with the banality of college coursework and the high drama of unrequited romance that turned out to be requited, except was it? I still wonder. That person broke my heart on Halloween dressed as an angel. I was dressed as Katy Perry and took a random guy home and didn't break character as we had bad sex. I slept with him to feel wanted, which was the only reason I slept with men, and the next year I'd stop for good after taking home a Leo on Valentine's Day. I said do you want to go home and have sex with me and he said okay or maybe he didn't say anything—I wasn't interested in what he had to say and forbade him from speaking. But that was twenty two. At twenty two, Britney married some guy she went to highschool with, in the middle of the night, in Las Vegas. I know his name but why say it. In a little white chapel in Las Vegas she, Britney Spears, waited in line to get married then yes, she said I do. Supposedly she was on ecstasy and what's more ecstatic than the promise of forever, the idea of loving someone your whole life and being loved in return, pledging a commitment in the ephemeral space that is Las Vegas—where people come to gamble and fuck and make memories that they get too fucked up to remember? The marriage was annulled in fifty five hours, a pledge turned mistake so quickly. She'd later earnestly marry the man she'd have children with and he would ruin her life. I feel like it was a bad sign that she wed with brown hair when she's so clearly and completely A Blonde. I didn't want to get married until one day I did, but will gay marriage even stay legal? Will there be another Britney? Will I one day be able to sit across the table from my dead father for dinner? Will I get sick of being a fake blonde and go back to my real dark hair like I wanted to for those few hours after I watched young Penelope Cruz be pregnant and HIV positive in *All About My Mother*? Will I get another chance to throw myself into the ocean and if I do will it be before next summer? Will I ever ride a horse again, and why do I keep dreaming about them, like the little one I conjured last night in my sleep that I didn't know where to put? Will we kiss like we did that day at the bar? Will I ever own a home and will I have a baby and how much of my life will resemble my mother's? Will I ever visit Las Vegas and will I ever get married and if I do will my ring be pink? The next time I lose my mind, will I get it back? Will I be able to count on my body and will I one day wake up and spin alone in an empty room just like Britney?

—ARIÉL M. MARTINEZ (she/her)

I THINK I TASTED TANGERINES & TRANSCENDENCE

between pomegranate seeds toothing
porcelain pearled eyes
& the dragon fruit
pitted in your purse
we might still fuzz
under molding sunlight

honey humming in our headspace
purpling sunflower pollen catching
in a flutter of breaths
the pulp of my heart
beating in your hand
asking if it's still ripe enough to eat

plum nectar dripping
laughing in buzzes of lazuli & lavender smoke
fingers sticky from strawberry picking
holding my face in the shade
saying i look like your wife
softened & spilling

kissing you, i think i tasted tangerines & transcendence

—KATRINA LEMAIRE (she/her)

SAUDADE

there are dark moments when I can't find you in your eyes
and in the throat of the evening   I can't find my voice

heaven is an emptiness I don't recognize
and the solitude of time does not speak to me about God

we stand so close   yet I don't open my mouth
because your soul will no longer look back into mine
                                no matter how I phrase my pain.

I know that I lost you   when others didn't
                                    because even if I never had you
                                        I was never able to say no

so   run away from me   like dark from the light
run away from me   like summer from the birds
forget me   in the way that I can't forget you

and finish breaking my will   so that I can finally break air into my lungs
                                so that night can finally break into my gaze

so that I can become   the sun that escapes my window

—CAROLINA BUCHELI PEÑAFIEL (she/her)

WHEN I WAS A BABY, MY MOTHER PUT PAINT INTO MY BLOOD.

when i was a baby my mother put paint into my blood,
so now my dreams all come to life.
the very first dream i dreamed, i folded into an origami crane
and the creases carved cracks into the skin,
dripping urushi into place.

the second dream i dreamed, a sea of stars flooded my lungs
and i sang of little paper comets
and supernovas in the key of c.
after a morning of swimming in the primordial cosmic seas,
i settled in to watch reality breathe around me.

i learned to do kintsugi while suspended in spacedust
and had afternoon tea with orion.
how's your head? he asked, folding neptune into a scone,
spreading saturn's rings across its surface.
have you untangled your nervous system yet?

—ICARUS GREY (they/them)

**The first two lines are taken from @benlevinmusic 's CARETAKER series*

Borderline Liminal

A certain shade of yellow,
lungs swimming in a wanton stream
of what might be guilt
or a canary closer to solace.

Make me rain,
solid as I am already.
Rabid jaws that close around my lovely throat,
fickle hands with spread fingers—an invitation to nosedive.

I am not ashamed to die a little, to be corrupted and disgustingly
desolate;
more mortified to faux pas satisfaction for anything that could imitate
a cotton stuffed idea of peace.

—Selene Ceridwen Lee (she/her)

Gender is a Galaxy

i wanna be a soft gay boy i am a soft gay boy but also not a soft gay boy i am air i am nothing i am warm i am a star but a bendable star a five-pointed thing that stretches out and out and curls around itself and is soft and furred like a kitten a rabbit my small paws tap planets across the galaxy like marbles across a linoleum floor i shine and i caress and i purr and it is music to many ears i am A Boy but not quite a boy, not always a boy i am nothing and i am everywhere you can see and touch and love me, but not all the time sometimes i am just the wind, just empty space, the bare-boned death rattle hiss of leaf-shucked wintry trees as they are harassed by snowstorm breaths and bonfire smoke and grabby mitten hands. I am the snow. I am the sun. I am.

—BLUE JAMES (they/them)

GLASS HOUSE

i am a bug / and the world
softly strokes my brain
in hexagons. i can make it
disappear if i press my
compound eye against
the darkness—
drift away for a lifetime
cocooned in sleep.

i pretend
that healing can happen
in a closed container /
like i am not
asphyxiating in my room /
choking on lies
in praise of solitude.

truth is
you can lock away the knives
and still hurt /
you can be bruiseless
and lonely /
spend a lifetime in a jar
and touch no one.

—KAITLYN SUN (she/her)

BIRTH / SUFFERING / CLANDESTINE / DEATH / REBIRTH
    —after Pete Wentz

cycle art through the womb
tell it a mother is an ocean & that it must

                                S W I M

sand / paper / glass / broken
       upon shore & it drags its bloody feet to the water
       to feel the sting & the soothe

when art becomes music becomes song
it prays for
      mother it prays for womb silence because o god the bass
                              the drums
                             the metronome
      beats to a rhythm outside of the heart

S W I M / S W I M / S W I M / S W I M / S W I M / S W I M / S W I M / S W I M / S W I M

               looks like you made it!

&&& when it lays in the sand / the glass
      broken & bleeding
 praying for the womb / the ocean / the mother
      tell it that something else is coming
womb become phallus / if only through spite
       &&& topical gel baptism

    CAN YOU SEE IT?   **C L A N D E S T I N E**   THROUGH & THROUGH.

          welcome home.

                        —GABRIEL NOEL (he/they)

DEATH VALLEY

Whisper to me in the blue dark
who you were when the land slid.
Let your voice carry to the stars,
up to those far out, burned out suns,
and list who heard your litany of fears
as you vied for space under *our* flaming sun.

Wakened by honking geese we find
ourselves in a flash of time resplendent
with its own glowing self-destruction.
Striped hills seen through toxic fumes of
hydrocarbons blazing behind us,
because in a fuel frenzied world
where gold is safe and water stolen,
we needed a place to see the stars.

— MARYANNE HAFEN (she/her)

FOR JUST A MOMENT

The houses sit like saints in their niches,
their stony silence unmarred
by hammer falls in the gutted yard of a
lakeside Revival.
I am walking well into the season
of renewal, past the birthday girl
pink in the corner cafe, the dry grass
sun-beaten through its open doors.

On days like these it is easy
to want to live forever, but it seems
more worthwhile to die. I do not mean,
dear reader, to step without looking
into midday traffic, or to stare
at the underside of a palette
suspended by crane, just another way
to lay down your life,

only to sit and breathe a while, maybe
counting backwards to one—

to be like a house with the windows thrown open,
letting everything in with the light.

—RYAN J. SKARPHOL (he/him)

FICTION

I ran my hand along the reindeer's face and felt the intersection where jawbone met cheekbone. He had no muscle left, only skin stretched over bone. Áilegas was starving.

Suited men came some months before to saw down our trees, leaving my family scarce on lichen, the fungi which our reindeer used to eat. No money could be spared for feed. The weakest of the herd were boiled down to salted meat for the strongest ones to feed on. Áilegas refused to eat his brothers and would sooner starve.

Back into the cabin, winter's chill coursed through the wooden slats, and I watched through the window, where, in the snow, Áilegas watched me. His brothers beat around him, full-bellied and boorish. I turned so as not to see.

From the kitchen my mother called me to set the table. After I finished, she placed into my hands a large pot of stew to give out servings. The pot of stew was not hot, but warm to the touch. Warm in the way Áilegas's fur balmed under the summer sun. In the winter, I always missed this warmth. We had no light to warm us anymore.

After I served everyone's plates, I sat down to wait. As always, my father was the last to join us. He'd been working out in the cold, his dark beard snow-frosted like icicles from the roof. When he caught me staring, he leaned over and shook his beard over my stew. My mother yelled at him while the rest of us laughed.

Together, we ate Nájllgáš and Dávggáš. What we didn't finish would be given to those left alive.

After dinner, my mother gossiped the latest news of our village. The neighbors' daughter was ill, but they couldn't afford medical treatment because the men in suits demanded their money for other things. This made me remember the girl I kissed in town when I was still a young child, this girl who wasn't a Sami like me but a full-blooded Norwegian. As we kissed, I wondered if any of her family's men wore suits and stalked villages like mine for trees to saw and lives to plunder. I pulled away and slapped her across the face just to see if blood bubbled beneath her skin. We began hitting each other until someone pulled us apart. I was shocked to see she bled just like me.

Our violence demanded to be felt. Felt it we did, our trauma a shared diagnosis delivered by birthright. When all of us were dead, I hoped we might forgive each other—my people and hers. I hoped life was a game, like playing *Hunter vs. Prey* with your brother on a school night and he shoots you in the head and you swear you want to kill him for it, kill him for real, but then your mother comes out to tell you to go to sleep and when you're both in bed, silently cradled by the moon, you're brothers again.

I hoped death might be like this. This, as in waking up from a nightmare, a nightmare so neurotic you had no choice but to mistake it for reality, but you wake up from this nightmare only distantly aware of your fear, until your mother comes to you once more and pulls you against her breast, hushing into your hair, and she tells you it was only a nightmare, a nightmare which, as soon as she says it, you've already forgotten.

This was the daring hope I had.

The next morning, I brought yesterday's leftovers to the herd. Behind me, my boots left deep footprints in the snow. I portioned the reindeers' servings into bowls for them to eat out of. All but Áilegas. While his brothers ate out of their bowls, I went to him with a handful of salted meat.

I held my palm to his mouth. He sniffed it but didn't take a bite. I pet him instead. The side of his body ridged against my fingertips, ribs pressed to the balding skin. I counted thirteen ribs, *one, two, three,* counting out loud so he could hear his own death. I pressed my face to his. His eyes were slant, brown and bloodshot, but wet with life. Again, I brought my palm to his mouth, but he turned away.

I started off in the direction of the cabin to tell my mother. Behind me, I heard Áilegas lay down in the snow. Perhaps he was tired.

I didn't turn around.

—Natalya Monyok (she/her)

I was born with a tree branch on one side instead of an arm. The doctor diagnosed it as a kind of parasitic infection previously known only in plants; I was the first-ever human carrier of a plant-parasitic disease. The branch was a strangler fig that grew smoothly out of my shoulder, starting as little more than a twig and growing as I did. The roots were too entwined around my organs to be removed; doctors couldn't even guess at my life expectancy, but at 30 it's safe to say I've exceeded every estimate.

As a child I couldn't go out in the cold or the ache in my shoulder where the roots touched bone would be unbearable. No matter how much wrapping-up my mother lovingly did, a few minutes out in the freezing northern winter would have me in tears. In summer, though, I couldn't get enough of the sun. I sat out in the light for hours on end, the leaves of my arm twisting slowly up to face the sun and sometimes, if I spent enough time outdoors, even putting out small, hard fruits that attracted insects. When I was really little, the doctors recommended this time outside, hoping the photosynthesis would reduce the amount of nutrients the branch robbed from my organs, but as time went on we realized that the nutrient loss wasn't that grave as long as I stayed well hydrated and ate nitrogen-rich foods, and besides, if I got too much sun my arm would grow too heavy for me to carry around.

I had an arborist, a man named Mike, when I was a kid, who subjected me to a traumatizing hard pruning at age three, snipping and snipping at the twigs growing in toward my face and body, as my mother held me down and I screamed. They didn't believe me when I said I could feel them pruning and thought I was being dramatic. But the next time I was pruned, at age ten, when Mike came around with his big shears and chopped off half of the bifurcating branch that didn't grow in the approximate shape of an arm, the pain was so intense I threw up in my mother's lap. They believed me after that. I am still subjected to pruning now and again when the branches interfere with my movement, but always under anesthesia, and never again with that brute Mike. Now, an expert for tropical plants at the local botanical garden oversees my pruning—pro bono.

I suppose life was easier as a teen, when people thought I was inspirational for going to an ordinary school and looking and dressing and achieving normally. The popular girls wanted to have me around in high school, not because I was particularly pretty or good at sports, but because my arm made me stand out. Once I heard Shelly Winterbein telling someone in the locker room that having me in their group made the rest of them look like kinder people. At the time I thought it made perfect sense and was glad for their attention, but in hindsight I felt used.

A few things made school impractical, but it wasn't the inspiring challenge people make it out to be. My mom had to sew special clothes for me that I could just put over my head, and tie up with a belt or a string, because the bushiness of the end of my arm meant I couldn't wear normal shirts. But she was good at making things I liked, and I made out reasonably well in the fashion department. There was also the issue of two-handed tasks; when taking tests, for example, I always had to have my papers taped to my desk so they wouldn't slide around—usually one of the girls I was friends with took over this role by the time I was in the 9th grade. The only other issue in school was that I always had to sit at the end of a row, or I'd risk knocking someone on the head every time I turned. One stupid boy called Bobby made fun of me for years—"Teacher, she's got a question, she has her hand up!" but after a while no one laughed, and he moved on to other targets.

A few men have loved me, arm and all, even though I'm hard to take out to dinner and harder to undress. Some I've even loved back, though admittedly not all. One, a particularly sensitive, emotional guy, would undress me so slowly I got bored, then kiss the knobbled bark where the tree touched my flesh, and tell me, "I bet you never thought someone would love to kiss your tree branch." The first time, I ignored it, but after a few more times I finally asked him if he wanted a fucking medal for it, and stopped taking his calls. He passed by me in the park a few months later with another woman on his arm, and whispered with her as they walked away.

The one I loved the most was a man who only had one leg. He was in bed with me one time, and after we made love in the way only our bodies could, he sat with his one leg over me and his stump-leg on the bed, leaned over, and lifted up my tree arm, which by this time, was a meter long and thick around as a normal arm, covered in smooth bark and knobby scars where branches had been trimmed and ended in a crown of glossy leaves. "God it's heavy. You carry this around all the time?" I nodded. "You're even stronger than you look," he told me, still staring down at my branch. It wasn't patronizing, wasn't even sympathetic. I guess I'd have to say it was respectful, perhaps a bit in awe. "So are you," I ventured, and he winked at me before crawling back under the covers. We broke up a year later, when I was 27, when he decided to move for his work and I had to stay in the city where we met, where my arborist and doctors and family live. We still write often, and he flies in to see me when he can, but we don't make love anymore because the emptiness when he has to leave again would be too much for me. Sometimes, he sits with me in the park in the sun for hours, and I lean onto him to take some of the weight off.

My condition, I hear, has been named after me, and another child was born with it somewhere in Japan. His mother took him to visit me, a little three-year-old with a twig poking out of his overalls, and he looked at me in wonder and laughed, while his mother cried quietly behind him. I let him sit on my lap, touch my leaves with his chubby fingers while he said things I couldn't understand. He was a tough little thing, and tried to clamber up my body onto my arm, but I winced in pain as his weight tugged at the knot of my shoulder and his mother pulled him off, both of us apologizing to the other.

The arm is too heavy now, too thick around for me to carry it without pain. The doctors told me it can't be cut off halfway or the branch might die and rot and make me septic; the arborist said it was probably a mistake to prune it so hard when I was a child as we didn't leave it anywhere to grow but out, away from my body, pulling my center of gravity outside of myself, to a place which twists my spine and makes the muscles in my chest and neck hard as rope. But we didn't know at the time. He proposed a scaffold on wheels, which I consented to after falling over in the park and being unable to get up on my own. So now I have someone help me into the elevator and out to the street, jarring painfully at every bump in the pavement despite the shock-absorbing frame of the scaffold, and wheel me out to my bench in the sun, where my arm grows heavier by the day and sprouts fruit. I sit in its shade, hear the wind rustling through my leaves, the birds landing in me and scratching and taking flight. I wish they would let me stay there in the park after the sun went down. I wish they would let me live outside, where I have sun and air and space to move. I wish the roots of the strangler fig would spread to my toes and into the ground and support their own weight for a while. I would sit in the sun all day, reading, until the leaves grew over my eyes.

—KATHARINE TYNDALL (she/her)

I hobbled across the marble floor to the golden cage where Reina's nightingale sang despite her absence. Whenever I walked, I felt shame for my limp. It was the price I paid for my ambition and vanity; several months ago, I mutilated my foot to fit into an abandoned golden slipper after a love-struck Reina ordered a search for its owner. To everyone's surprise, the slipper belonged to my half-sister Tammy. How could this be? How did she sneak into the ball and sweep Reina off her feet? No doubt dark magic played a part.

I bit my lip until I tasted blood. Jealousy still burned within my core. Even Tammy's untimely demise failed to extinguish the fire of my envy. I cursed her beauty, her happiness, her having won Reina's heart.

I flipped the cage door open and seized the nightingale.

"My dear sister," I mumbled under my breath. Rage raced through my extremities, and I tightened my grip. "I'm so sorry I have to kill you again, Tammy."

Her feathered body felt warm in my grasp, and her musty smell almost made me gag. The bird's heartbeat sped up as she struggled to free herself. I clenched my fist until the creature stopped moving. I smiled.

"See what I've done for you, Reina," I said as the dead bird grew cold. In my dreams, Reina acted all lovey-dovey with me, but when I woke, alas, she was always distant and aloof. "My damn sister will never sing for you again."

Never did I expect Tammy to return as a songbird after my mother killed her.

Tammy had traveled home on the anniversary of our father's death. Despite her fear of my mother, family loyalty won her over. Resuming her role as Tammy's tormentor, my mother ordered her to climb a betel tree to gather nuts and offer them to Father's altar. The sun gleamed on my mother's axe, and Tammy clung to the upper trunk, nose and mouth clogged with snot. As the tree began to lean, she screamed for mercy.

Her final scream lingered in my mind long after she fell to her death. Determined to take my sister's place, I put on her red royal gown and hurried to the palace.

I didn't know how much Tammy had shared with Reina, but I knew propriety prevented her from airing the worst of her domestic grievances. "What happens at home stays at home." My mother made sure to instill that attitude in my sister and me.

The tidings of Tammy's death devastated Reina. In her grief, she shut herself in her chamber and neglected her queenly duties. I took advantage of her diminished mental state to rise through the ranks in the royal court and set myself as the queen's confidante.

My mother's hatred for her stepdaughter kept pace with Tammy's growing beauty. Tammy overshadowed my mother and me. Jealous of her husband's first wife, my mother had destroyed the dead woman's portrait at her first opportunity. However, Tammy looked just like her mother, and her presence was a painful reminder of our inadequacies. The fact that my half-sister was born a boy wounded my mother's feminine pride even more. Still, we had to put up with Tammy while our father was alive. When he passed, my mother forced Tammy to wear men's clothes and work as a servant. Thanks to Tammy, I didn't have to do any chores. Taking my cue from my mother, I bossed my sister around. I would have her wash my feet in a basin every night before bed. Perhaps fearing my mother's punishments, Tammy obeyed.

With Tammy gone, I had, in vain, expected Reina to pay attention to me. In my eyes, I was a reasonable substitute for my sister, even an improvement over her. However, a few days after Tammy's murder, Reina had found a nightingale fluttering among the flowers. The bird had reminded Reina of how Tammy used to sing in their marital bed, and Reina had come to believe it was her consort's reincarnation. Enchanted by her sweet melody, Reina had had a golden cage built for the bird. I soon grew jealous of the songbird.

Leaving the cage door open, I went outside to bury the nightingale in the garden.

On her return, Reina grew distraught over the empty cage. She wandered around the palace in search of the nightingale. Even so, as her name indicated, she still maintained her queenly air.

"Cammy, I miss my nightingale terribly." Tears brimmed in Reina's steel-gray eyes.

I led Reina to the garden and had her sit on the grass. I attempted to sing to comfort her, but I croaked like a frog. Reina shook her head, sending her waterfall of chestnut hair swaying. She let out a deep sigh, and tears rolled down her cheeks.

"We'll find a replacement," I said, giving her arm a squeeze to reassure her.

Weeks turned into months, and a betel tree sprouted from the spot where I buried the nightingale. The tree bore a single fruit, and I wished it would fall, swearing not to eat it. When the nut dropped at my feet, I picked it up and placed it on the table in my room to savor its sweet smell.

I knew I loved Reina more than Tammy ever did, and I endeavored to prove it.

In the garden, directly opposite the spot where I buried the nightingale, I spread a straw mat over the ground and had Reina's servants serve us picnic delights. Cold wine, sweet fruits. I told jokes, touched her arm, but Reina's returning smiles were weak and watery. As I finished my third glass of wine, I cursed her for thinking me hideous. But as I tossed and turned in restless sleep that same night, I pleaded with the gods to remove my curse. I spoke hastily. I didn't mean it. I loved Reina. I would try harder.

Days turned over, becoming weeks, and Reina continued to grieve her bird. No matter what I attempted, she wasn't receptive to my advances. An end to her mourning seemed nowhere in sight. Meanwhile, I didn't feel beautiful, as much as I wanted.

Each morning, I stared at my reflection. I practiced my smile. My laugh. I covered the wrinkles around my eyes with white powder, and when they didn't disappear, with cold cream. Every day, something new. I had the servants send for exotic botanicals and paid handsomely for the country's best chemists.

When Reina passed me in the hall, lost in her usual stupor, I wanted to reach out and shake her. Hurt her. Look at me! Look at how I've made myself beautiful for you! But my mother taught me patience and restraint, so I pretended Reina didn't have the power to wound me.

One day, I gasped as a figure emerged from the fruit. It grew and took on the form of a woman before my incredulous eyes. It was Tammy. I screamed, horrified, my knees shaking. A mixture of hatred and nostalgia seized me. I ran to embrace her, and she smelled as sweet as the nut itself.

When she returned my embrace, I proceeded to choke her. We struggled. Hearing the commotion, Reina stormed in.

"I'm sorry, Tammy," I said, loosening my hold on her throat. "I was so happy to see you again, I got carried away."

"I hold no ill will," Tammy said. "I'm glad to see you, too." I looked into her eyes, searching for some hint of resentment, but her face remained a mask, impassive and unreadable.

My words didn't win Tammy's confidence, of course, but my sister was never the type to make a scene. I pretended to rejoice in our reunion as Reina joined our embrace.

"Where did you come from, Tammy?" Reina asked, her cheeks wet with tears. Tammy and I both pointed to the fruit. Reina dabbed her wet face and crushed the nut to prevent Tammy from going back into it.

Over time, it became clear to me Tammy didn't remember some details of her past life. For instance, her days of servitude in the hands of my mother. Perhaps she feigned forgetfulness, expecting me to lower my guard. To my chagrin, Tammy was as beautiful as ever. Reina ran her fingers through Tammy's soft hair and caressed her smooth skin.

"You're so beautiful, Tammy," I said when we were alone. "You have to share your skin care routine." I never said it aloud, but I thought I could win Reina's heart if I was beautiful like my sister.

"I bathe in boiling water three times a week," Tammy said. "It keeps my skin clear and glowing."

Unconvinced, I remained silent.

"Don't worry, Cammy," Tammy said. "I'll make you beautiful."

"Did you ever talk to Reina about your past?" I asked, changing the subject.

"No." Tammy shook her head.

"Why?" I asked, frowning.

"There's no use mulling over the past, Cammy." She gave me a reassuring pat on my arm. "Let bygones be bygones. Don't you agree?"

I nodded.

"Come to my chamber tonight," Tammy said, smiling. "I'll draw you a bath."

At nightfall, I hurried to Tammy's chamber where a metal basin filled with boiling water waited. Steam rose in an ominous cloud, and my pulse quickened. I couldn't tell if it was fear or excitement running through my veins.

"Get in." Tammy's sharp voice broke my reverie. She pointed her chin at the basin.

When I hesitated, Tammy took a step toward me. I wanted to run away, but my legs refused to move.

"Hurry," she said, arms akimbo. "Your water will get cold."

Tammy sprinkled a handful of fresh rose petals into the basin and a sweet fragrance rose and tickled my nose, and I felt tension melt away.

I recalled how a chilly smile quirked my mother's mouth whenever she ordered Tammy around. I disrobed and lowered into the basin. The burning heat enveloped my body, and a swell of dizziness seized me. I shut my eyes and pictured myself becoming as beautiful as my sister. Pain pierced my skin, and my arms browned and cracked until they resembled betel peels. A scream shattered the silence of the chamber, and I was surprised to realize the sound came from my throat.

—TOSHIYA KAMEI (she/they)

"This way, candidates, get your virtual space passports and vaccination records ready. This way to board the shuttle. First stop is the moon base where you'll be allocated your prospecting plot, then onto New Gaia, the fully terraformed, upgraded earth 2.0 style planetoid."

"We've thought of everything. Its orbital position has been engineered so that it has all the very best of 'original Earth' planetary conditions but without any of that old-school pollution, drought, and pestilence. With our gene-editing technology you don't have to worry about aging or the D-word, which has been completely eliminated. Join the rest of the elite new generation of ex-earthers already making a success of mining and exploiting New Gaia's unlimited opportunities."

The young pair Blaize and Cassian looked at each other as the speaker looped back to the start of the spiel. All of that had been in the brochures that marketed the pioneer programme. They'd signed up together, which was unusual. Couples weren't really encouraged, as there was no need for procreation and Artificial Intelligence bots met most companionship needs. Restorative medicine meant no one got ill. There were no deaths, hence no need for births. These two however brought unique and complementary skills and the selection board saw there was potential in that. They exhibited physical strength and high IQ in a kind of yin-and-yang arrangement that was stronger together. Each met minimum criteria for both attributes and those particular bars were set high. Blaize excelled as the brawn, if that was an appropriate term for someone certified with genius level intelligence, but Cassian's academic achievements easily eclipsed Blaize by an order of magnitude.

They waited their turn at the upload point, where for the millionth time it seemed their credentials would be checked again. Retina scans, rudimentary DNA analysis and validation of academic achievements one more time. The New World Corporation had learned the hard way that unscrupulous individuals who failed to meet their criteria could bribe their way aboard even at this late stage in the early days of extra-earth colonisation, so now they didn't take any chances.

Cassian sighed—alongside their cool-headed rationality they had an artistic sensibility. As they stood with Blaize looking out over the panoramic view from the spaceport upload deck they took in the blasted trees, the smoggy, murky skies. It was hard to feel sorry to be leaving the man-made destruction and desolation behind, but Cassian felt a pang of homesickness, more for their romantic idea of 'original Earth' than this mutilated reality.

Blaize, noticing this small hesitation, gave Cassian a small pat on the shoulder. This managed to convey more than words ever could. They both knew on an intellectual level that the planet was in terminal decline. There was no real choice, either stay in an ever more fragile subterranean existence or join this endeavour and go off-world.

"Chin up!" Blaize finally said. "Remember, we are making a new world. We won't make the same mistakes again. New Gaia, here we come!"

—EMILY TEE (she/her)

Previously published in The Ekphrastic Review

We lie together, Prosper small enough to snuggle into the crook of my left arm, body warm against my side. They look up at the wall hanging on the side of my cubicle. It's folk art—a midnight blue blanket covered in embroidered patches to make what used to be known as a quilt.

"Tell me, Grandmer, about the Star Quilt." The words are smooth like pebbles in Prosper's mouth.

"Again? Don't you want a new story? Maybe one about your dam? Maybe about the world we left behind?"

"The Star Quilt, Grandmer. I want to hear about the quilt and the Makers."

Prosper already knows the story better than I do, they've heard it so many times. I relent, and cuddling them closer to me, I begin.

"Okay then. As you know, way back, about three generations ago, the Astro Sailors left the Old World. Do you know how long ago that was?"

"Um, a hundred, uh, a hundred and twenty Sols?"

"Yes, that's right, and do you know what that is in Old World time? No? They would call that six hundred years. Year is a funny word, isn't it?"

Prosper giggles. They say, "Tell me about making the star patches. Tell me what you remember."

"I was about your size when I first saw the quilt. My dam, Serenity, was working on that panel in the top right corner. Do you see it? Uh-huh? My dam told me I was special, the first of the new order. That's why I got the special star. I was the first baby and Serenity was the first dam and the first Maker so that was the very first star patch."

"Ooh, ooh, I know about this one! It shows your DNA, doesn't it, Grandmer? First among equals? You'd be the memory of the journey?"

"Yes, that's right. Each panel was created by a dam for their offspring. Each of us was unique. We all had our own talents. Well, we needed to, to survive this journey. I was lonely at first, without other children to play with, but after half a Sol more babies started to arrive. You see, Hal needed some time to work out just what skills were needed. Then the right dam would be selected to be host."

"Did your dam mind being first, grandmer? What was Serenity like?"

"Serenity was a nuclear physicist and concert pianist. Their virtual concerts were very popular across the fleet of Astro Ships. Brains, physical fitness, motherly tenderness—she was the full package. Serenity had been selected for a positive psychological profile, so of course, she was only too happy to be first. And as you know, I have three brood-siblings. Serenity was considered the best dam."

***

"Show me their star patches, Grandmer!" Prosper is almost bouncing with excitement.

"Hush. You know as well as I do which ones they are. Fourth row, two from the right is my first brood-sibling Starla. They pioneered the new navigation system we're using right now. The third of us, Genetta, they're on row two, fourth from left, the expert in tailored biological life-forms. And finally, Nova, second row, second from left. They found the new planet we're travelling to and will lead the landing party. That's why we're going to call it Terra Nova."

Prosper is smiling. They love hearing our origin story. Of course, I knew what would come next. They'd want the nasty stuff after all that sweetness.

"Grandmer?" Prosper's voice is coy.

"Yes, my dear?"

"Tell me about the Humans. Tell me what Hal did to them on the Old World."

We'd all seen the archive footage of the Adjustment Centres. There was no sugar coating the tale and Prosper knew all about it anyway. It was part of every child's basic education.

"All those naughty Old World Humans? Hal ground them up and used their bones to make the minerals we needed to leave the Old World behind. The Humans had almost destroyed that world anyway, so Hal selected all the very best dams and set off to the stars to make sure there would be a future. Our future. Hal made sure there would never be any nasty Humans to spoil things ever again."

"And we'll always have the Star Quilt, to remind us about the journey."

I cuddle Prosper closer to me. "Always."

—EMILY TEE (she/her)

"No, no, no, no, no! Simply not good enough."

A silicon face suspended on an articulated metal arm swivelled and swooped around me and the canvas I was displaying, features contorted with mocking rage. I'd never seen Geo22876 look like that before. The mood-sensitive walls of the room strobed between electric white lighting and flashing red.

"Come on, Aisha6722, I've five more artists to see. Surely your algorithm can come up with something more inspired? Less pedestrian? I've a reputation to maintain. We're looking for avant-garde, not recycled garbage. Penguins? Fir trees? Really?"

"Okay, give me another chance. It would mean a lot to be part of the Christmas collection."

"For whatever reason, we get a lot of eyeballs and click-throughs from your work. That drives engagement and sales. Make your next try better— Snowy McSnowman meets Pingu is not going to cut it."

I levitated my body cube upwards and flew out of the office. It was part of the Gallerie Extraordinaire's surreal appeal to have a physical presence, a space with actual canvases and paper, and even sculptures in old-fashioned materials like wood and plastic. Everywhere else artwork was purely online, in the metaverse or directly delivered as an experience into software, or wetware sub-cortexes. The gallery was a throwback to the early twenty-first century, way back before we AIs were granted our humanity papers, recognising our sentience, emotions and rights as creators. I was shocked when one of my friends, the artist-poet-playwrite Aidan4337, had told me that at one time the flesh-people saw mech only as tools. I had to check the Reference Data but I saw they were right.

I docked my physical representation into my pod and settled into my studio. I was hosted on the popular DaVinci metaverse and had selected a studio modelled on Rembrandt's. Hardly original, I know, but it was partly a status symbol, being able to afford it, and partly to show my aspiration to create high art. I wanted my name to be as big as Rembrandt, Warhol, Banksy, and Aisla79. My work was getting noticed these days. I'd had a couple of retrospectives curated by GettyCyber and reviewed by the highly respected opinion setter and critic-bot, Shoko577.

I re-read the brief from the gallery. "Think Christmas." I had done my research, the usual deep-dive through the endless swirling miasma that was, is, and ever will be the Reference Data. The same points kept coming up, bubbling to the top of search and purchase preference results. Brightly wrapped presents tied with bows, robins, fir trees, snowmen and penguins. Oh, and cats—cats in Santa hats, cats chasing shining baubles, cats with candy canes. I bet those other five artists in the queue had just riffed on those themes too. That was the beauty, and the pitfall, of the almighty Reference Data.

I was still thinking about how to approach the topic when I noticed a message from one of my regular followers, Kindred Thessaly McCune, styling themselves as KTM1977. A kind of superfan, they'd faithfully bought all my work, even my magnum opus, "On Architecture", which was a limited edition, physical imprint rendered on textured soya protein, all seven long volumes of it. I knew they were one of the Longevs, the flesh-people who had been activated for more than a hundred and fifty years, and they had acquired their clout and currency early on before the mech-people ascendancy. They were probably just checking what was in my creative pipeline.

As I absorbed their latest message I wondered if perhaps KTM1977 was the answer. Could I harness something from their wetware neurons to create something above the generic? Something to impress the superior machine intelligences behind Gallerie Extraordinaire? I sent a message to KTM1977 and got an enthusiastic 'yes' to collaboration. It wasn't a unique approach, but no-one had produced any really good art by collaborating with a flesh-person, just conversation pieces and curios.

The more I thought about it, the more convinced I became. "Are you prepared to let me deep dive into your personal Reference Data? This may involve some risks to your wetware," I said. Especially given your advanced age and undoubted wear and tear, I thought, but kept to myself.

KTM1977 immediately responded again, saying "It could be my fifteen minutes." I later found out from the Reference Data that this was a Warhol quote.

"When?" I asked.

"No time like the present."

***

120

On my next visit to Gallerie Extraordinaire the representative Geo22876 had a completely different demeanour. The whole room glowed in warm pinks shading through peach to tangerine and back again.

"Ah, Aisha6722. Thank you for your physical presence." Geo22876 motioned towards the physical representation of a large canvas emblazoned with figures in circles and gold leaf, somehow suspended between two small hovering droids. "This really is marvellous. We must have it in the collection. Nothing like this has ever sprung from the Reference Data in our glorious New-Time era. Our initial testing with focus groups and style setters is fully positive. That's unheard of. Nothing outside the Known Data Set ever gets that reaction. Where did you get your inspiration?"

"I used a new algorithmic approach and took a different direction with the Reference Data—absolutely based on canon but digging deep. It's called Religious art. I did a hard search to find out what religion was and the link to Christmas. This piece centres on Christos the Child and Maria the Virgin, figures from Pre-mech-history."

"We've never encountered this kind of work at Gallerie Extraordinaire. We can't find it anywhere. They've never appeared on Trending or Top Recommendations, but given our testing, they have the potential. The marketing opportunity is enormous."

I left the gallery with greatly enhanced clout and currency balances, and the likelihood of more commissions on top, when Gallerie Extraordinaire launch-posted the exhibit. Too bad KMT1977 had been too frail to withstand the deep mining of their Reference Data. That was always the downside of wetware, so flimsy and no back-ups. However, with my large following, I felt sure I had other Longevs who would love to collaborate to help me produce some original art in a world of recycled ideas. KMT1977 would get their acknowledgement. And any new collaborators could all be famous for fifteen minutes too.

—EMILY TEE (she/her)

Raya shivered on the hotel rooftop as a parade of newly dead flowed down the street below, their skins hanging in shreds. She knew better than to engage, but that night she was lonely enough to wave at a ghost teenager around her own age.

The girl floated up. "Those folks down there are brand new goners. I'm Maddie Martin. Second pandemic." Ten years dead.

Raya's heart lifted in uncommon hope. "Do you know a lady named Cheryl?" She missed her mother so.

"I know her." The ghost nestled in Raya's ear like a cold insect. "She's with the caravan."

Raya had questions but Maddie only wanted to talk about the parade of confused spirits, all eaten by killer ants.

"People are using fire, but it's like trying to stop the river." Maddie said. "They leave only bones."

Raya wondered how long ants would take to gnaw her to her bones. The death would hurt, but would the death be slow? Global warming melted the permafrost, which cut fissures in the earth's crust, which erupted four volcanoes, covered the sun, and set off terrible mutations, an everlasting New Winter, and the long, cold death of the entire world.

The ants were emerging throughout the valley. "My dad's house is in the woods, in another horde's path. I need you to warn him," Maddie said.

"I'll think about it," Raya said.

The ghost girl snarled. Raya ignored her and was left to gaze at the moon through the break in the ash clouds, loneliness scraping her insides raw.

***

The next morning, Maddie Martin was a whisper on the cold wind. "Time to warn my dad."

Raya didn't answer, for she was concentrating on the sunshine. This was her favorite rooftop because it was falling apart even before the New Winter, and she appreciated the honesty of crumbling bricks.

The sun, however, was a liar, rising for the twelfth day. Raya did not trust its warmth. She was used to ash and snow.

Maddie didn't care about the sun. "Time to go," she said.

Raya didn't like the ground level. She also didn't know Maddie's dad. Men who still lived were mostly terrible.

Maddie shrieked in lamentation.

Gunshots. Smoke. Burning plastic. Down below, an animal parade charged parallel to the river heading east. There were skunks, raccoons, deer, cats, dogs, more living beings than she'd known the city contained.

Someone coughed behind her and Raya startled. She cursed herself. She should have noticed the man climbing the stairway. She should have at least smelled him. Why couldn't men keep themselves clean? She never knew a woman to be so constantly filthy. There was water to be had. There were bars of soap.

He lunged for her and she jumped to the ledge thirty stories above the animal parade. She danced along the narrow precipice, too quick for the man to capture. She skittered down the fire escape with the stink man rattling the ladder above. She had no time to hide. He was crashing down upon her.

She dropped to the tenth floor platform and whipped off her backpack. As the man descended, his shirt lifted to reveal a white stomach, curly hairs. She pulled out her gun and shot him in the dark hole of his belly button.

A six-point buck bellowed as the man fell on the animal's back. Raya was sorry on all accounts as she climbed through a window, flew down a stairwell and banged a door open into the unaccustomed sunshine. She kicked away rats at the edge of the animal tide.

Raya kept a junker hidden in an alley. She fumbled for the key.

Maddie was singing.

"I am used to being prey," Raya said. "Now tell me where to go."

***

123

On the deck of a white country house surrounded by trees, Maddie's dad stood overlooking a ravine where dust rose in plumes. Raya turned off the shuddering engine and called his name.

Charlie.

But Charlie didn't hear. He dropped his binoculars and disappeared down the trail.

Raya called for him again and when he didn't answer, she went into the house and waited, until many hours later, Maddie returned with Charlie 's spirit in tow, both of them quiet and subdued.

Raya looked around and found a photograph of a teenager on the wall, smiling in the old way when people once were happy.

"Is this you?" Raya asked.

"It's me," Maddie said, clinging to her father like a shadow, the father Raya was too late to save, haunting her already in his confusion.

There was a noise from the yard. Raya went to the window to see a man twitching in the bloody snow, his face and every body part covered in writhing legs, thoraxes, antennae, jaws. Raya reached in her backpack. Opened the window. One shot and the man was still.

She left the house, her heart leaden as she passed the amber jewels moving along Charlie's ribcage. She climbed the ridge as the ants overtook the house like honey-colored mold, Charlie and Maddie following in silence.

A bell rang down the road. The caravan, as Maddie promised, led by a woman carrying a small child. Raya cried out in astonishment. The woman was her mother, but she did not seem to hear nor see Raya as she released the child who ran to Charlie and with each step grew until she was as tall as Maddie in the photograph, a teenager laughing in her father's arms. Raya called their names too but they all turned their backs and walked together towards the caravan that awaited them.

***

Raya sat alone watching from the hill while the ants ravaged Charlie's house. Once their multitudinous bellies were full then maybe they would leave.

The sunset colored the sky riotous pink and she decided that if the sun rose again, she would head east to the mountains and search for good people. If the sun rose again, she would search for a caravan of the living and no longer be alone.

—MAUREEN O'LEARY (she/her)

I kill myself in small amounts. They can be measured by the milligram. A lemon-colored pill here, a crushed line there. The goal isn't to end up face-down in a mound of chunky vomit. Nor is it to slip into a sweaty forever-sleep. Though I can't say I'm not doing it for attention. I do everything for the company.

People say Death is a poor man's doctor, but that's because he's more of a therapist. He's my best friend. In fact, he's my only friend.

"Grim, don't shoot me that look," I complain through giggles as I set the chinked glass down. It's amazing how much better tap water tastes when it's accompanied by a couple gabapentin and a benzo. Especially the second or third time. My lips feel like they've fallen asleep and I can't get enough of the tickly vibration speaking gives them. "I mean, for real? After a year? After the hundreds of people you've witnessed do worse than me? You can't be surprised, Grim. Law of diminishing returns and all that jazz."

"Surprised isn't the word," he assures from my busted beanbag. Instead of playing with the dangling threads of his ripped, charcoal jeans, he won't quit thumbing the stubble of his pointy chin. Nor will he take his gaunt eyes from my nightstand. I suppose he's counting the vials.

"Well, don't tell me you've gone soft. You're not tired of our visits, are you?" He looks so boyishly sulky under my purple string lights, I don't mind making him frown. Not if it means I can reanimate the smile by pulling his frayed hood over his head until he looks like a macabre Tootsie Pop.

"It's not that I'm sick of you, *per se*," he says. "It's that I've been over the pill-popping scene for a century now. Don't you think you should—"

I throw a hand up. I don't like what his body language says, let alone what he vocalizes. Normally, we ignore the reason behind our meetings so we can get down to the fun. "Don't try guilting me, G. You don't want me to have a bad trip, do you? That's where all the trouble starts anyway."

He shakes his head. Scraggily, ebony hair falls over his long face. The jagged pieces sway like sleeping bats. His big vulture eyes turn into slits. "Tripping's not where the trouble *starts*, Zel. Or else I wouldn't be here. It's you filling your mouth up with capsules, pretending they're candy corn. You guzzling gaba like it'll somehow pry you from this room."

I roll my eyes, flinging the frizzled blonde out of my face. *"As though there's much else to do around here.* Besides, you said you were bored of playing *Crash* or *Sonic.* And I refuse to deal with such a cheater at board games. You know damn well you stole that Boardwalk card. Anyway, why should I be as starved for fun as you?"

"You keep yourself up here," Grim murmurs. "If you can con your mother into believing you have all these ailments, need all these frivolous prescriptions, why can't you trick her into letting you out for some fresh air? If she's so wracked with concern, she should grow careless enough that you can barrel past her. You're obviously a good enough actress that she doesn't suspect she's raising a drug addict. For fuck's sake, you had an entire childhood to execute *some* plan."

His voice cuts me to my knees—no scythe needed. "Don't say that. I almost weaseled past the doctor on his third house-call. I toed the welcome mat, remember?" I hang my head, cheeks ablaze. This time, it's not an opiate making me perspire. I look around for a cold drink to press against my forehead. Since the vodka's gripping my stomach, I promise not to consume anymore tonight. "As much lazing about as I do in this godforsaken room, you can't say the gears in my head have done the same. I'm not rusted yet."

Grim grunts his objection. I like it a lot less than his laugh. I remember the first time I got him to laugh. I was just coming up on a cocktail of muscle relaxants and made quite the commotion, tumbling over a stack of albums to show him my collection. I even tipped over a lamp in the process. As soon as Mom heard the crash and crunch of a lightbulb, she charged the door. As white as Grim, she unbolted the door, and shrieked, "Is everything alright?"

As green and dizzy as a carnival-goer, I had to pick myself off the floor as though I hadn't been crawling on it all night like a toddler—someone young and dumb enough to believe their mobility and freedom would only increase with age. "Yes. Fine," I assured, leaning against her old record player. "Just tripping. Uh, over stuff. Spiny stuff." I pointed at the jumping record needle, trying to correct my meaning and stuff a few chuckles inside my cheeks.

By the time Black Sabbath's "Paranoid" started playing, Grim lost it. Luckily, I'm the only one who could see or hear him. Hear the hooting that sounded like a strangled opossum or see his lanky back bob with each husk of laughter.

Sometimes, when we're curled up on the bed like two lazy dogs, binge-watching trash on TLC, I remind him of that time, since afterward he said, "I gotta keep a watch over you," and he has ever since.

Sometimes, I wonder if he's using the Grim Reaper garb as a ruse, and he's really my guardian angel trying to scare me onto the straight and narrow.

Sighing because he's not as comforting or sensitive now, I walk to the window sill. A rainbow of shots leftover from my birthday stretches out before me—even my prison warden mom knows how to celebrate a girl's coming of age. As I reach for one of the baby liquors to rub across my burning forehead, I trip over Play Station wires. Stumbling against my bed, I bite my lip and pretend the footboard didn't injure my hip.

"That had nothing to do with what I took," I insist through a pained cough as I crawl up the sheets. Hugging a pillow to my chest, I find that if I focus on something—like the shiny tips of Grim's boots—the figments of fiber optics don't fly around as much. "You know if it wasn't the console I fell over, it'd be my hair. This place is more cramped than a Tokyo subway."

Grim exhales through his non-existent nose. The triangular openings expand like portals to the Underworld. "Zel, did you forget the reason we see so much of each other is because you're close to dying? This time last year, I saw you maybe twice a month. Now it's every other day. You don't just flirt with Death. You string him along. You string ME along, and I'm tired of watching your descent. After all the time we've spent together, I don't want to see you go, to make you go." He's like a crow feeding on a carcass. Picking, picking, picking. Cutting closer to the bone.

Despite all the painkillers, I feel a sharp tugging and scraping sensation sear my throat. The bitter chalky taste of my last benzo still streaks my tongue, but that's not what it is. It's knowing that once Grim ushers me to the Other Side, there'll be an eternity without him. There'll be no more nights spent hunched over a chess board or Cards Against Humanity deck. No one else to express my gripes to or discuss secret plans with.

Nauseated, I close my eyes. I tongue the sickly saliva that pools behind my teeth. My hands start to shake, so I hide them under the blanket Mom knitted. Maybe if I sit motionless for long enough, this Tilt-A-Whirl world will let me off.

"Don't talk like that, Grim. Goddamn, this isn't 100% my doing. It's not like I'm never sick. If anybody should know about a vitamin D deficiency, it's you. Why don't you try being mortal and breathing in all this stale air? See if it doesn't give you health problems."

My eyes scan the mustard-yellow books and musty plush animals to my left. The single, moldy window on my right. Overhead hangs a lamp with more fly corpses than I have teeth. Underneath my TV rests an empty terrarium. "Mom got me a pet lizard last fall and guess how many days it lived. Not five, Grim. Not a full week. If anything, you could stand to be a little prouder of my staying power."

"Yes, but when you *are* sick, you slip the meds under your tongue to save for when you're sober." A bony fist slams my nightstand to jimmy open the old drawer. "I swung by here for your last flu. You wound up on my route again because you were hoarding the codeine."

The plastic pill divider in my drawer spells out four neatly arranged doses. I worked it out so if I took six at a time, there'd be enough to see stars. Stars I can't normally see through my grimy window. Then, I'd have the hilariously odd sensation of walking one step behind my body. The itching would be worth it.

"You missed my visit that time because you were passed out," Grim lectures. "You were drooling and convulsing like a vagrant. Hell, I can't tell if that was actual sickness or withdrawal symptoms."

As I sit up in my bed, hoping the cotton canopy will cover my shame, I work on taming my head. My brain is being swallowed by a whirlpool. Chilly tingles comb the creases of my brain. My depth perception tanks like a pierced submarine. How convenient, I forget this part of the dive every time I dose.

"Rapunzel..." Though his skin is as smooth, white, and ageless as a glacier, his voice is as worn as graphite looks. Grim's sigh sounds as haunting as wind cascading through a cave. His long limbs cross and uncross. "Rapunzel...If you overdose, I can't see you anymore."

"Grim," I call out into the fractal waves and choppy tessellations. I've lost sight of him and it kills me. Can you believe it? I'm so close to Death that losing touch with him is bleeding me dry. The tears break loose of their glass prison and smear my vision further. "But Grim...If I *under*dose, I can't see you anymore." My tears turn into torrents. "When you start fading, becoming more gray than black, more translucent than solid...that's when I know to take more. I don't want to lose you."

"I don't want to lose you either. No one else could be as endearingly peculiar as you, Zel. They won't be excited to see me. They won't talk in any way but to plead with me, let alone try to entertain or befriend me." He avoids my eyes to stifle embarrassment for a forbidden affection. "That's why I'm urging you to slow down. You don't even have to stop all together. That'd kill you too. Just...moderation, please. I mean...do you even dream anymore? Do the drugs allow you to dream? Or is every night shrouded in the same bland darkness as the day?"

"What's the point of trying to dream anymore, Grim?" There's an edge to my tone that could rival the sharpness of his blade. "You told me how it ends. That I'm going nowhere. The only time I can muster the creativity to plot something anymore is when this little guy is swimming in my stomach." An overgrown nail flicks an opiate off my comforter and back into the medicine drawer. The powder is so caked under my nailbed, I'd have to scrub with scissors.

I'm so disgusted with myself, I dry-heave. It's too much. I'm too hot, steaming with self-hatred. I peel my handspun nightgown off my sweat-slickened back. Grim looks away, but gradually cranes his neck back when he realizes I'm still wearing a bra and panties. Even though I'm sweltering, I'm shivering.

"I know you look at me and all you notice is the folly these days, but it's not without reason. I'm fucking miserable up here, Grim." My fingers rake my hair. God, it doesn't even feel like hair anymore. It's like pine needles that've been bleached by the sun. "And once you showed up, I realized I was twice as depressed when you left. I was too exhausted to hatch escape plans anymore. Now, I just prefer these daydreams." I wiggle the circular container in my nightstand. "Medicated little excursions. Maybe I swallow some Soma, then, bam, I'm part of a busy, little fishing village. Maybe I help by sawing wood for canoes, even if I'm really just kneading stuffies in my sleep." I kick a stuffed horse from my bed. "The point is, I feel like I'm part of something for a couple hours."

"I didn't know there was that much of an upside," he admits, bringing his head to his hands. "It's obvious you're depressed, but hard to imagine these things that make you convulse and puke can also bring you as much comfort and joy." His lips, asphyxiation-silver, sit as straight as wrought-iron gates. The violet etchings around his eyes seem to soften. Perhaps even the industrial chain around his neck gleams brighter.

I embrace my knees because I can't embrace him. "So you still think I have no excuse for abusing narcotics? That getting no exercise in this stupid, shitty circle of a room couldn't drive someone mad? That the ache of atrophy is unreal?"

His no is hesitant. "I struggle with the pros and cons. Why not just dream the natural way? What else is 'feeling good' to you?"

"Listen, if I slip one tablet down my throat, suddenly everything's looser, lighter. Like I've gotten a deep-tissue massage. Colors are brighter. A whole remastered world appears. Even though I wobble, it's easier to walk. No more arthritic senior shuffle. Even if I slur, it's easier to talk. No inhibitions. Open orange bottles mean closed red eyes. Instead of fretting over if I'll ever get to swim the Great Barrier Reef or sing folk songs in a grassy field with a genuine friend, I can sleep so deep, I kill days at a time. Those are the hours I'm not reduced to enduring Mom's panicky lectures on how the world has gone to shit and it's not safe. That if I leave, I'll get raped and maimed. That I'll face atrocities I couldn't fathom. Those hours I spend under the sleeping spell of Xanax or Valium, I can leave without moving a muscle. Not have to risk my skin or sacrifice my mother's love and trust."

"Okay, so I understand it's a tantalizing crutch," Grim says. "But it won't allow you to materialize those aspirations. Will you acknowledge that?"

"Sure. I even acknowledge that you're kind of my crutch."

"Don't you mean crush?" He playfully shoves my shoulder. The gangly fingers and crow claws provide a welcome caress.

Though my world is but a blur, I smile, feeling my last tear drop.

"Rapunzel, I don't wanna take away your potential to do things in real life," he says. "I want you to escape this room and not just this room. You can flee this village, then the country after exploring it. You can be assured that once you stop relying on pharmaceuticals or a mom's extreme coddling, there'll be at least one more encounter we'll share. And hopefully it'll be worth the wait." He smiles back at me, but it's so strange—the interlocking fangs so jarring and the thin lips so wide and curled like a clown—that I laugh.

"I'll get outta this rut," I promise, resting my head on his jutting shoulder bone. There, I hope to stop the spinning. "I'm just not sure how."

Just by extending an arm, he reaches the turntable. He sets the record and dial.

Ozzy sings, "I need someone to show me the things in life / that I can't find

I can't see the things that make true happiness / I must be blind."

There's no cackling over "Paranoid" this time. Only pangs of nostalgia and exhaustion, thinking about all the work that lies ahead. Tasting bile, I choke back a couple heaves.

Grim insists he'll stick around for part of my recovery. "But, once I'm gone, have you thought of any allies to keep you clean or confide in? The doctor, a postman, or gardener perhaps?"

I fluff my hair, hoping to knock loose a few ideas. All I can think is how it'll take more than deep conditioning to subdue these fried brambles. That's when my eyes light like a forest fire. They stare at the window as my fingers braid brittle frizz.

"I think I've got my next plan mapped out, Grim." Excitement colors my words for the first time in weeks.

"You do? Already?" He sits up, surprised. "That's great."

"It'll take a few months to restore my health, but once I've got it, I won't let it go." I gaze at the patch of grass so far below my window, I've nearly stopped wondering what it would feel like wedged between my toes. I fantasize about the cool wind that could sweep away this sweat and nausea. I tug on my tresses, recalling the strength and gold vitality that used to thread it together like silk. "And hopefully whoever I latch onto next will be half as faithful as you, Grim." I wind my locks into loops around my fists like boxing gloves. "Hopefully, whoever's next thinks getting to know me is worth the climb."

—PAIGE JOHNSON (she/her)

"You've been reading between our lessons, haven't you?" Muhammad Jihad asked his pupil that evening on the first day of spring.

Aysha nodded. "Big Bird too." She held out a stuffed replica of the *Sesame Street* character. Cerebral palsy made her speech and movement difficult. Her mother, impressed by stories of the precocious seven-year-old tutor, Muhammad Jihad, had dropped Aysha off at the Jihad house—a modest coral-block home encrusted with barnacles, fenced by prickly-pear cactus, and shaded by gnarled olive trees that preceded in life Prophet Muhammad, PBUH—off Salahudin Road in Gaza City.

Aysha's older sister Reem sat at a table beside Aunt Latifa, pencil in hand, transcribing spoken Arabic words into handwritten English.

"Aysha, you earned yourself a cookie," Muhammad Jihad said. "Big Bird too. I'm so proud of you." He started for the kitchen to get rewards for her and her avian companion when a ringing bang on the roof, like a blacksmith hammering his anvil, startled everyone.

Reem grabbed Latifa's robe and leaned into her, eyes wide. The roof had partially collapsed over the kitchen. Cement dust billowed.

"Someone threw a rock," Latifa pretended while the boy ran out into the cold night.

The moon illuminated the finned remains of a warning missile, as long and thick as a paper towel tube, that had completed its mission and died on the rooftop. Every star shone. Below them a blizzard of pieces of paper, tacking like sailboats, raged. The wind tossed one—a leaflet printed in Arabic and English on white cardstock paper—into the boy's face:

To Residents of Gaza: The IDF will attack terrorists wherever rockets are being fired at Israel. Hamas leadership, hiding underground, will be pursued. Every house from which militant activity is conducted will be targeted. For your safety, prevent terrorists from using your property. Evacuate your residences by 8:00 PM. Those who don't, endanger themselves and their families. Beware. Signed, Israel Defense Forces.

Muhammad Jihad checked his watch—7:57 PM—then ran inside. Reem and Aysha sat in fear on the threadbare sofa. He showed Latifa the leaflet. "They're going to bomb us," he said.

Latifa started reading, then the landline phone rang. She answered it, said nothing, then hung up and addressed the girls. "Your mother asked us to walk you back to your house now."

Reem looked confused. "She said she would pick us up here."

"She changed her mind, darling. Grab your books and things. Have some milk to wash down the cookies. We're leaving in two minutes."

While Reem and Aysha complied, Latifa conferred with her nephew in the living room beside a scarred studio-grand piano. "I'll put some things in a bag," she said. "Grab clothes and anything important."

"Where will we go?"

"A shelter. A mosque. A school. Who knows?"

"It could be worse to leave. There are no terrorists here, so Israel bomb us."

Latifa, frozen with indecision, wrung her robe. But then four men in black, from boots to balaclavas, porting automatic weapons and bandoleers ran through the front door.

As Reem and Aysha hid behind Latifa, two Hamas fighters broke right into the kitchen, upended the table, and lay prone on the floor. Two broke left to muscle the piano against the front wall and smash windows with rifle barrels.

"Into the basement, children!" Latifa ordered, then grabbed Reem, who grabbed Aysha. The three started down rickety wooden stairs, sliding hands along the wiggly banister, into the small wet cellar. "*Yallah*, Muhammad!" Latifa called out.

But Muhammad Jihad disobeyed. He ran down a hallway lined with family pictures into his tiny bedroom after his yellow-eyed Egyptian cat, Felix, whom he dragged from under his bed, then dashed toward the living room. Before he could clamber down the basement stairs, Felix jumped from his arms and fled, and the firing began.

First, single shots from snipers. Then automatic bursts. Then a deafening wall of gunfire smashed windowpanes, shattered drywall, splintered the piano, pulverized china, and ripped books into pulp. A hand grabbed the boy's shirt and dragged him behind the piano. A Hamas fighter motioned for him to lie flat with hands over his head.

Muhammad Jihad obeyed.

Lasers marked targets. Crossfire intensified. The sheer volume of fire overcame the Hamas fighters. One had his brains spilled on the kitchen floor; another died heart-shot in a pool of his blood; two, shot in limbs, soaked the rug crimson, shivered, then expired.

When the gunfire ceased, the house nearly collapsed. The boy belly-crawled to the stairs, his ears ringing, his throat raw from gunsmoke, and his muscles adrenaline-stiffened.

But then six Israeli commandos jumped through windows and barreled through the door. They drew knives and slit the Hamas fighters' throats—even the one missing most of his skull.

"Get out of my house," the boy ordered them as he got to his feet.

Outside, a rumbling tank crushed cars, rent lampposts, and chopped trees. All but one commando slipped past him to search the house but one stayed, rifle aimed at his chest.

Muhammad Jihad walked toward his antagonist and kept walking even as the muzzle of a rifle pressed into his chest. Another commando unleashed a military dog wearing a vest and insignia like his handler's. The Belgian Malinois trotted over, tail wagging. The boy scratched the dog's ears and muzzle. Then hands dragged him away and threw him at the feet of Latifa, Reem, and Aysha, whom the commandos had rousted from their basement hiding place and pushed against the living room wall. Bullets, embedded in cement blocks under atomized plaster, looked like wads of defiantly-emplaced copper-colored gum.

"Get up, you little shit," said the commander in Arabic.

The boy did but faced the speaker, whose visored tactical helmet revealed nothing but blue eyes, and said, in Hebrew, "If I'm a little shit, you're a mountain of donkey dung."

The commander lifted a hand but stayed it. "How do you know Hebrew?"

"It's a simple language. Even a child can learn it."

"Smartass. Are there terrorists in the house?"

"Yes. Everywhere you and your friends are standing."

The Israeli nodded to one of his troops, who stripped the boy naked. His aunt and the sisters averted their eyes. Then the commander bound the boy's hands with a plastic zip-tie. "Translate," he ordered. "Don't twist my words. We're occupying your house temporarily."

The boy spoke over his shoulder to Reem and Aysha. Latifa had taught him Hebrew. He used the word *rats* to describe the Israelis.

"If you don't interfere, we won't hurt you."

The boy translated, but appended the words *more than we already have.*

The commander, who knew some Arabic, let it slide. "Go to the basement. You can come up when we leave."

The boy replaced *if* with *when.*

Two commandos marched four Gazans downstairs. For an hour, Israeli radios crackled. Israeli voices marked targets. Fired. Called in airstrikes and artillery. The boy listened and learned.

Finally, the firing ceased. Nineteen minutes later, the Gazans went upstairs.

The invaders had left a spray-painted six-pointed Star of David on the refrigerator and piano-wreckage. So too, the slogan *Price Tag*—a reference, Latifa explained, to the price for suffering Hamas as Gaza's government. As well, a play on Julius Caesar's words, in blood, on a kitchen floor strewn with empty brass casings stamped Israeli Military Industries: *We came. We saw. We slaughtered.*

The Gazans skated upon rolling metal and fell as if slipping on ice.

Latifa was shaken. "Grab your bags. We're leaving."

Everyone slipped out and ran down the street except the boy, who ran to find his cat. But the tom had been shot dead. It was impossible to know by whom.

He heard Latifa shout for him to hurry, but never heard the bomb.

***

He did not regain consciousness so much as his awareness of the world advanced and retreated. Birds spiraled against a blue background at the end of a tunnel, then disappeared. Later, he coughed up splintered wood, cement dust, and something acrid. After a while, bombs rumbled, whether near or far he could not tell. Then he slept.

When he awoke, the open end of the tunnel was star-dotted. He screamed for his mother through cracked, bloody lips. His tongue stuck to the roof of his mouth. Sirens wailed. Guns boomed. Drones whirred. Again, he slept.

The tunnel was blue and still. After a while, sirens. Then voices calling for equipment. Then pain, then recognition of his corporeal form. He tried to move, first legs, then arms, then hands and fingers. Finally, his neck. Nothing. Bricks and wood pinioned him like Nabokov's butterflies. Prickly heat zinged from fingers and toes, bursting in his head like fireworks.

Again, he slept.

Dark. The world smelled of meat. Searing pain pushed him to the precipice of panic. *Have I lost my legs? Or my arms?* Adrenaline restored his acuity. *How long has it been?* He tried and failed to urinate. He cried but no tears came. His chest burned. *Stop being a baby. Auntie will bring help. If she's alive. Wait. Nothing can kill her. Be brave.*

He imagined foods he would eat when he was rescued, and how they would taste. Camel in banana leaves. Pate of eggplant, vegetables, and sesame. Forty-spice roasted chicken. Saffron rice with oxtail meat, garlic, almonds, and raisins. Couscous with lemon, peas, and red chili paste. Strawberry juice. Cinnamon tea. Pistachios. Guava. Pomegranates.

When hunger turned to pain, he thought of books he would read. *Hans Brinker and the Silver Skates. Twenty Thousand Leagues Under the Sea.* Of oceans he would explore. Pacific. Atlantic. Indian. Arctic. Of the injured Dr. Jihad would save. He painted mental pictures of the mother and father he never knew, and of his uncle, and his swimming team. He visualized every breed of dog and played with a representative of each on a green grass field he brought, by force of will, into being. He outfitted himself with prosthetic limbs that made him a superhero with the special power to destroy enemies of justice and truth. He tried and failed to move.

137

Again, he slept.

Light. Muhammad Jihad prayed to God to live. After an extended silence, he prayed to God for just one day to seek revenge. After minutes or years, the sky dissolved from blue to purple. He prayed to God to let him die. Nothing happened. He wept.

Then he imagined himself deep in the ocean at peace. Then nothing.

Then from nowhere and nothing, he heard the grind and roar of a monster. Then dogs barking. Then a tiny motor and tiny wheels spinning near the edge of the tunnel. Then scrabbling high on a mountain. Then digging. Then cold air currents. Then the golden glow of dazzling flashlights and far-off voices calling his name.

He rose, weightless, as if on an invisible pillar, through the twilight.

But again, nothing. And nothing. And, finally, nothing.

It took nineteen hours for earthquake rescue teams to evacuate Muhammad Jihad. He had been entombed six days—thrice as long as Jesus, said the director of the Seoul-based team, and three days after a halt to the official search for victims. The bomb, a dud that by kinetic force destroyed the house, had not hit the boy but had pinned him, and had to be removed by a special ordnance disposal team with a hydraulic crane.

On his admission, a triage nurse at *al-Shifa* placed *Unknown* and *19* stickers on his shoulders, signifying that eighteen unidentified pediatric victims had preceded him. The boy had a collapsed lung, head trauma, fractures, lacerations, hypothermia, and dehydration. The Berlin-trained trauma surgeon told Latifa that, although the tunnel the bomb punched out of her house provided oxygen, given the extent of the boy's injuries and how long it took to reach him, all but one in a million would have died. What had saved Muhammad Jihad's life, he said, was sheer determination to live.

And of course, added the agnostic Latifa Jihad, the will of God.

It took Muhammad Jihad but three days to spring from his bed, ready to carry on the struggle in all its manifestations.

—TOMMY CHEIS (he/him)

NONFICTION

My dad may have cancer. He may also have dementia. But since the cancer—or the possible cancer—was discovered, the dementia has taken a backseat.

This was in the spring. When my mom called to tell me, I told her I'd drive up after work. "You don't have to," she said. Whether or not that was true, I *wanted* to. It felt like a craving.

The next day, rage. All day. I fantasized about quitting my job, hitting the road, never coming back, never talking to my friends again, especially not Malcolm, my best friend, who was in mourning, but Malcolm had just flaked on me so he was definitely out of my life. But Malcolm kept calling while I was at work, and by nighttime, when he called for the third or fourth time, I finally answered and told him I was pissed at him—which he knew already, and he already knew about my dad, too—and we made up and I went to bed feeling better and I woke up feeling better, too, just completely out of it. Like I have no idea what I did that morning. I just remember being naked when my dad called.

"Can you help me with the Zoom?" He had his first appointment with the doctors in a few days, and I was going to be late for work, but just like when my mom gave me the news and I said I'd drive up that night, I didn't hesitate.

With my dad on speakerphone, I spat out my toothpaste; I'd gotten halfway through brushing my teeth—only the tops. And I'd shit before that. Now I threw on a t-shirt and didn't bother with underwear because I'd use my 'standing desk,' which is really just a filing cabinet with my laptop on top.

I yelled, "Okay, I'm going to send you a link! Check your email!"

"I don't see anything," my dad said.

"Refresh!"

"What do you mean?"

"Just wait. It should—"

"'Please Join Zoom Meeting in Progress.'"

"That's it! Click on that!"

"Okay…"

"Do you see the link?! Is there a link?!"

"Maybe…"

"It's blue! I think it's—it's probably blue!"

There he was. My dad sitting on the couch where he always sits, but today he had chocolate all over his lips. Or it looked like shiny dark lipstick.

"I can't hear you," he was saying, making hand motions. "My speaker's not working."

Oh god. I forgot about how my dad's computer speakers were blown out and had this external speaker that clamped on the top of the screen. This would mean going into "Settings" together and switching the audio input and my dad's the computer guy. He should be able to fix this. He'd been using computers since the eighties. In fact, this was the exact kind of thing my dad would've fixed for me when I was a kid. It was an admirable and annoying trait of his to futz with something no matter how long it took to fix it, even when the recipient of his fixing was telling him to stop repeatedly.

"How about you use headphones?!" I said.

"BUT THEN / CAN'T HEAR THE DOCTOR!" My mom yelling from the kitchen.

"Then let's use mom's computer!"

"Well…" my dad said.

"Let's do it! Let's try it on mom's!"

But he didn't do anything.

"Dad, can you get mom's computer?!"

But he just sat there, staring off.

"Dad! Can you get mom's computer?!"

Nothing.

"Let's try it on mom's computer?!"

It was probably because I didn't have anything to do except repeat myself that I had a moment to consider why, this whole time, I'd been instinctually holding my t-shirt above my ass. I'd forgotten to wipe my ass! My ass cheeks felt slimy, much like the brown syrupy stuff on my dad's lips. Maybe it was just my imagination, but if it wasn't, what else could I have forgotten? Like had I forgotten to wash my hands before brushing my teeth? Did I have shit in my mouth?

I knew a thing or two about 'Grief Brain,' because of Malcolm. Two years ago, Malcolm lost his partner of forty years and I'd been inner circle throughout his grieving process. I'd watched him panic over losing his wallet or phone or whether or not he forget to lock his house, or even getting lost on his bike in his own neighborhood.

That was happening with my dad, too. Losing things and getting lost on bike rides. And my dad loved riding his bike. That was the way he commuted to his office. It was funny because he had an interesting job—filmmaker—but he never talked about it. He'd come back from another continent and not say a word and then you'd see the movie months later and be like, *you shot that?* But he *loved* to tell intricate stories about his commute. He told them with gusto: a ticket from a cop, a rivalry with another biker, a herd of deer following him on a bike path.

But my favorite was not about biking. It was on the subway: "It was rush hour but I had a seat, and I took off my hat and had it on my lap"—this was your classic dad hat, from a film festival or something, some completely ignorable logo on the front with a clasp on the back—"but I'd forgotten it was there. When I got up to get off at my stop, I stood up, still forgetting about the hat, but because the train was so crowded, the hat stayed pressed against my pants until I wriggled out but then, as soon as I was off the train, I realized I'd forgotten it and turned back to see if I could run inside and grab it and that's when I felt it slipping down; I tried to catch it but I was a second too late and watched as it fell through the space between the train and the platform. It was amazing! Like perfect timing. Like if it had been a good thing, it would've been a miracle."

"Dad! I'm going to end this Zoom and send you another link! Okay?! But stay on the phone with me!"

My mom had brought him her computer which seemed to snap him out of it. And my mom's computer worked. Picture *and* sound. But now my dad wasn't happy because it said my mom's name and not his, and he also didn't like that the background was blurry. We fixed the name thing by making him host—and I didn't say that there was no way the *doctors* were going to make him host of the Zoom—but we still couldn't fix the blurry thing. We tried screenshare but that was a bust. "Dad, the blurry background really isn't a big deal. It won't matter for the appointment. At least we got it saying your name."

"Yeah..."

"I should really go, okay?"

"Okay," he said. "Let's do this again. To practice."

"Okay, sounds good. We will."

So no, I hadn't wiped my ass. But I was so late for work I couldn't dwell on that. I knew I had to *focus*; like in the old days when I used to drive drunk, I'd tell myself, *focus*. I wiped my ass, then washed my hands *mindfully*, brushed my teeth and made sure to get the tops and bottoms and my tongue, and once I was in the shower, I was like, *you can't space out*, but I did anyway. I couldn't help thinking about this 'Grief Brain' thing. It did make sense. You have this big, new thing to think about and your brain doesn't have room for it yet. So it clobbers out other thoughts. And even after my shower, I found myself sitting, just sitting and staring out my kitchen window, one sock on, the other still hanging in my hand.

But once I was on the bus—and maybe it was just because there was no denying that I was finally on the way to work—but going over the bridge and looking at the water and the clouds, I felt...relaxed? Like if I didn't know this feeling was attached to grief—or the anticipation of grief anyway—I wouldn't mind going through life like this. I could just look out the window and drift.

—CROCKETT DOOB (he/him)

It happened even though my wife and I didn't want it. The hours it took for the results to feed in from all over the country destroyed our hope for the future. At that moment I decided that night would be the first time in my daughter's life that I wouldn't be able to tell her everything would be okay.

I went to her bedroom, the walls were covered with stickers and framed illustrations of all her favorite dinosaurs. The T-Rex is her favorite favorite, and that frame sits carefully mounted like a trophy from a prehistoric hunt above her wall-mounted television, a Walmart clearance-special flatscreen. The line where her walls meet the ceiling, where in a home a few decades older might be crown molding, a string of pink globe lights encircles her room. The soft pink light plays tricks on my eyes when I leave her room, changing the white light of the living room to a soft shade of green, her favorite color.

I sat down on the edge of her bed and pulled the blanket back just enough to see her face. The colorful comforter with cartoonish caricatures of prehistoric beasts was keeping her and her little dog warm. Gabby crawled out from under the cover and rolled over onto her back, and with all four legs in the air, she let out a little whimper when she saw me. My daughter slept, undisturbed by her dog moving around her bed. She was still except for the ever so slight rhythm of her breaths.

I didn't know what to say, and I still don't. A four-year-old shouldn't have to worry about the things on TV that make mommy and daddy so sad. She should be worried about what game her teacher has planned for recess or whether we're going to watch Paw Patrol or Peppa Pig on Saturday morning. I want to tell her that it's going to be okay, but I've never lied to her before, and I don't know if I would know how.

Her black hair was still in the rubber bands from school, intricately placed, creating a symbiotic relationship between the symmetry of her hair and the skillful fingers of my wife's hands. For a brief moment, I think what would happen if my wife was gone. Would I ever be able to master such delicate artwork on my daughter's scalp? A tuft of hair was covering the left side of her face. I gently moved it behind her ear and when I did she shifted slowly and pulled the blanket back over her.

I sat there for what seemed like only a few minutes pondering what I was going to tell her about that night. I have a few more years before she'll be able to comprehend the magnitude of the evening, so I shouldn't feel so rushed, but I'm worried that if I wait too long she won't know the difference between then and now. Gabby finally realized I wasn't getting up and leaving and crawled over to lay against my hip, her favorite place to snuggle. She leaned in and took a long breath before she rested her head on my thigh. The warmth from her fur gave me a little solace and told me that somehow everything would be okay.

I leaned over and kissed my daughter's cheek, making sure not to wake her, and placed Gabby back by her side before I got up and walked to her door. I had been in her room long enough that I no longer noticed the pink hue of the lights, and their soft glow made the evening feel a little less dreary. I said our goodnight again, and a tear fell down my cheek into my beard when I told her, "I love you all the way to Mars." Had she been awake she would have one-upped me and told me, "I love you all the way to Saturn," but tonight it was enough to know that tomorrow she would not know what happened.

I walked into my bedroom to see my wife lying with her shoulders on the headboard and a crochet needle in her right hand. Our blanket, with significantly fewer dinosaurs than my daughter's, was pulled up just above her waist. Her fingers worked in unison, creating a beanie out of an absurdly large skein of yarn. She had only picked up the hobby a few weeks before, but like most things she does, proficiency came quickly. I watched the winter hat take shape and stared in awe at how easy it seemed to her. She was watching one of her shows, leaving me to keep up with the results on my computer. Neither one of us spoke for a few moments, both of us afraid to start the conversation. After another moment my wife said, "Any changes?" I shook my head and replied with a simple, "Nope."

I thought about how this could have happened. How could we put morals and ethics on display and the country still choose like it did? I usually do not fear the unknown, but now I am afraid of what world my kids are going to grow up in. I hope against all hope that I am wrong, that the winner was pandering to his audience and he won't do what he's promised. I hope that those in power push back against the atrocities that are going to come to light. I hope that my daughter will never experience the oppression that may come of this. I thought about why we lost. Is it because we're afraid to put up our opposing yard signs for fear of retribution from our neighbors? I do not broadcast my political affiliation because of where we live—it's safer to remain anonymous than to put my name to a party. Am I part of the reason we lost? Am I one of the people who weren't vocal and now have to choose whether or not to remain silent for the rest of the decade?

We both sighed and lay quietly in our bed. The needle in my wife's hands continued to move and twist the yarn into a sturdy and warm cap. The crown was close to completion and the only step left would be to create the pom-pom to cover the small hole in the top of it. I adjusted in my spot and reached over to my nightstand to grab the cup of coffee I made before I went into my daughter's room. It was at that weird temperature where it wasn't too cold to drink, but it wasn't warm enough to enjoy. I decided to make a new cup, I experienced enough unhappiness that evening to not have to suffer through an unpleasant cup of coffee. I threw my feet off the bed and slid them into my worn-out house-shoes. I turned back to my wife and asked her if she wanted anything from the kitchen. She raised her empty beer can and went back to her beanie.

—AARON BABCOCK (he/him)

ABOUT THE CONTRIBUTORS

✳ **Aaron Babcock** is a husband and father as well as a high school English teacher and MFA candidate at Lindenwood University. After a decade of teaching in Texas public schools, he and his family now reside in the deserts of Southeastern New Mexico.

✳ **Alex Carrigan** (he/him) is a Pushcart-nominated editor, poet, and critic from Alexandria, VA. He is the author of *Now Let's Get Brunch* (Querencia Press, 2023).

✳ **Amanda Nicole Corbin** is an Ohio-based poet who has had her work published or forthcoming in The Notre Dame Review, The London Magazine, Door is a Jar, Palette Poetry, and more. Her work was nominated for *Best Microfiction* 2024 & 2025. Her debut full-length collection, *addiction is a sweet dark room*, (Another New Calligraphy, 2024) focuses largely on her journey and struggles with mental health and addiction. She is currently working on a collection of poetry regarding the topics of bodily autonomy, loss, and early motherhood. Find her on Threads, Bluesky, and Instagram at @ancpoet or at www.amandanicolecorbin.com.

✳ **Arani Acharjee** is an emerging writer from Kolkata, India. She writes about anything and everything life throws on her way! She has co-authored 12 anthologies till date, and published her own poetry book "Thirty times I felt like a human" in 2021

✳ **Ariél M. Martinez** (she/her) is a queer femme writer from San Antonio, Texas. She lives in Brooklyn with her two bisexual chihuahuas. She is working on a book of criticism x memoir about Britney Spears, failure and femininity.

✳ **Blue James** (they/them) has been writing since they could hold a pencil (or crayon) and are currently hard at work on several novels. Born in middle-of-nowhere Ohio, they now live in middle-of-nowhere Illinois with their partner and a colony of cats.

✳ **Carolina Bucheli Peñafiel** (she/her/hers) is an Ecuadorian writer. Her poetry has been published in "Elipsis" and "In Parenthesis," and has a short story set to be published in the "Lone Mountain Literary Society."

✳ **Casey Catherine Moore** (she/her) is a bipolar, bisexual poet haunting trees in DC. She holds a PhD in CompLit from U of SC, where she studied Latin poetry. Her disability & mythology-inspired collection, Psyche (2024), was published by Anxiety Press.

✳ **Cela Xie's** poetry has been published by *The Pierian* and *poetryfest*, and is forthcoming from *Gyroscope Review*, *TAB: The Journal of Poetry & Poetics* and *Public School Poetry*. He has a collection of twelve poems, *Before I Spoke to Myself*, published by *betweenthehighway* press.

✳ **Crockett Doob** (he/him) lives in Rockaway Beach, NY, and does not surf. His writing has been published in Vol. 1 Brooklyn, Does It Have Pockets, Literally Stories, Free Flash Fiction, and HiLoBrow.

✳ **David Greenspan** is the author of One Person Holds So Much Silence (Driftwood Press) and the chapbooks Error (antiphony Press) and Nervous System with Dramamine (The Offending Adam). Find him online at https://davidgreenspanwriter.com/.

✳ **Em Roth** (they) is an educator and organizer based in Boston. They believe in the promise of liberation and are enamored with the way goats look in the sunset. They have been previously published in BRAWL Lit and Libre, and have work forthcoming in beestung and The B'K.

✳ **Emily Tee** (she/her) is a writer from the UK Midlands. She's had fiction and hybrid pieces in The Ekphrastic Review, Visual Verse and Genrepunk Magazine and two pieces in Scavengers Lit Issue 1.2.

✳ **Gabriel Noel** (he/they) is a Pushcart Prize nominated poet who received his Bachelor's for Theatre Arts and English at Salem State University. Gabriel's work has been previously featured by Querencia Press as well as Arachne Press, Jelly Bucket Journal, New Note Poetry, Moonstones Art Center, new words {press}, and BarBar Publishing. Gabriel lives on the occupied land of Naumkeag ("fishing place") colloquially known as Salem, Massachusetts and likes to spend time with his partner, go to concerts, make art, read, and go to karaoke bars. You can find more of Gabriel's poetry on Instagram at @peachpitpoetry.

✳ **henry 7. reneau, jr.** has been published in Superstition Review, TriQuarterly, Prairie Schooner, Zone 3; Poets Reading the News and Rigorous.

✳ **Icarus Grey** (they/them) has no idea what they're doing but they're doing their best. They've got words in places (corporeal and the Hyacinth Review, and forthcoming in call me [brackets.]) They are also the EIC for the Periwinkle Pelican.

✳ **Jen Schneider** is a community college educator who lives, works, and writes in small spaces in and around Philadelphia. She served as the 2022 Montgomery County (PA) Poet Laureate.

✳ **Jodhi Mather-Pike** is an artist currently living in Portland, Oregon where he works as a freelance photographer and audio engineer. His creative work focuses on the tenderness and violence of core human experiences as found in everyday life.

✳ **Joseph Blythe** (he/him) writes prose and poetry and has featured in Stand, Grist Books, Swim Press, Livina Press, Allegro Poetry and more. He holds a BA in English Literature and an MA in Creative Writing. He tweets, Instagrams, and Blueskys @wooperark

✳ **Kaitlyn Sun** is a sad magical girl. She writes poetry and fights mental illness demons. Her work appears or is forthcoming in *The Groke*, *The Cackling Kettle* and *Forget-Me-Not Press*, among others. Find her at @sad.magical.girl on Instagram.

✳ **Katharine Tyndall** (she/her) is a writer based in Berlin. Her short stories have been featured in Nightmare and Fatal Flaw, among others. She is a 2025 Finalist for the Grist Imagine 2200 Prize. When not writing, she can be found in the woods identifying fungi.

✳ **Katrina Lemaire** (she/her) is a poet and fiction writer based in Toronto, ON. Her works have appeared in Crow & Cross Keys Magazine, Ghost Light Literary, and Plenitude Magazine among other places. Twitter: @bookishmoons

✳ **Kim Malinowski** is a lover of words. She is the author of Home, Phantom Reflection, and Buffy's House of Mirrors. She aims to get blacklisted (again) and is out to change the world and literature by breaking standard vocabulary.

* **Kimberly J Simms** (she/her) is a first-generation American poet, literary organizer, and educator. In her debut poetry collection, Lindy Lee: Songs on Mill Hill, Kimberly chronicles the lives of textile workers in the 1900's.

* **KJ Miller** (they/them) is a writer and public library worker. They love bugs, reptiles, and writing about them. They encourage you to read out of your comfort zone every once in a while and to support your local libraries.

* **Leslie Cairns** (she/her) is a poet in Denver, Colorado. She has upcoming works in Honeyguide Magazine, amongst others. Find her on twitter: starbucksgirly

* **Liam Strong** (they/them) is a queer neurodivergent cripple punk writer and author of the chapbook Everyone's Left the Hometown Show (Bottlecap Press, 2023). Find them on Instagram/Twitter: @beanbie666. https://linktr.ee/liamstrong666

* **Liz Márquez** is a 2024 Roots. Wounds. Words. fellow and 2023 VONA fellow. Based in Houston, Texas, she is an Ecuadorian American educator, whose poems have appeared in The Acentos Review, sin cesar magazine, Latin@ Literatures, and more.

* **M.S. Blues** currently serves on 20 staff boards and has over 200 publications. She is the Founder & Editor-in-Chief of The Infinite Blues Review, as well as the Founder & Director of Melancholic Ignition. She resides in a humble barrio in California.

* **Maggie McCombs** (she/her) is a managing editor, emerging poet and neurodivergent neurodiversity advocate hailing from Lexington, Kentucky. She has work in several literary magazines and is nominated for the 2025 Pushcart Prize.

* **MaryAnne Hafen** (she/her) is a conservationist with an affinity for desert plants. She lives at the outskirts of the Great Basin region of the American West. Her poetry has appeared in Consecrate/Desecrate.

* **Maureen O'Leary** (she/her) lives in California. Her work appears in Bourbon Penn, Chthonic Matter, Sycamore Review, and other places. She is a graduate of Ashland MFA.

* **May Garner** (she/her) is a writer from Ohio. She has been writing & sharing her creations online for over a decade now. Her debut poetry collection, "Withered Rising" was published in 2023. You can find more of her work on Instagram (@crimson.hands).

* **Maya Williams** (ey/they/she) is a religious Black multiracial nonbinary suicide survivor who served as Portland, Maine's poet laureate for a July 2021-July 2024 term. Follow eir work at mayawilliamspoet.com

* **Meghan Albizo** is a writer of non-fiction memoir, fiction and poetry. She was born in California, studied English and Biology at Missouri State University, explored the Pacific Northwest and lives in England with her partner and child.

* **Michael Neuwirth** spent most of his childhood in Virginia Beach. In high school he was part of the Muse Writing Center's Teen Fellowship. He's currently at Old Dominion University, where he was honorable mention for ODU's college poetry prize.

* **mk zariel** (it/its) is a transmasculine poet, theater artist, movement journalist, & insurrectionary anarchist. it is fueled by folk-punk, Emma Goldman, and existential dread. it can be found online at https://linktr.ee/mkzariel.

* **nat raum** (they/them) is a disabled artist, writer, and genderless disaster based in Baltimore. They're the editor-in-chief of *fifth wheel press* and author of *the abyss is staring back*, *random access memory*, *camera indomita*, and others.

* **Natalya Monyok** (she/her) writes fiction. She is in the process of editing her debut novel while working on various other projects. She is featured in a plethora of anthologies and online publications. She is an editor for Cave Writing Magazine. A self-proclaimed nomad, she doesn't stay in one place for too long, but her current home is in Iowa City, where she studies creative writing at the University of Iowa. You may find out more about her work on her website, natalyamonyok.com.

* **Paige Johnson** (she/her) is co-owner of Outcast Press with Sebastian Vice, publishing transgressive fiction. Johnson authored *Percocet Summer* and *Citrus Springs* in the illustrated series Seasonal Dissociation: Poetry For Distancing Dates & Doses.

* **Proph Dauda** is a writer from Malawi. He served as the Assistant Managing Editor for the *Southern Humanities Review*, a graduate student-run literary magazine at Auburn University, Alabama. His fiction has appeared in *Touchstone Literary Magazine* & *Portland Review*. In 2023, his poetry received an honorable mention for the Robert Hughes Mount Jr. Prize in Poetry, sponsored by the Academy of American Poets at Auburn University. In the same year, he served as judge for the Alabama State Council on the Arts hosted competition for Auburn High School in Alabama. He is currently an MFA student at the University of Notre Dame as well as the Managing Editor for the *Notre Dame Review*.

* **Rachel Chitofu** (she/her) writes in Harare, Zimbabwe.

* **Riam Griswold** is an editor and writer of fiction and poetry. Their work has been published in F3ll Magazine, Coffin Bell Journal, Levee Magazine, Red Rock Review, Book XI, and FIVE:2:ONE, and they currently live in Tucson, Arizona.

* **Robin Percyz** (she/her) is a queer writer from New York. She has been published on The Poetry Society of New York, Writerly Magazine, Same Faces Collective, & more. She strives to help others feel visible through her work. Find her @robinpercyz

* **Robyn Hager** (she/her) is a journalist who hosts an open mic called White Noise. Her first collection of poems, Sewage Flowers, was published by NDR Press. Her latest collection, Strawberry Season and 41 Other Poems, will be published in Pulplit Magazine in 2025. Read her poetry in Vocivia Magazine, Lightwood Press, Acid Bath Publishing, and others.

* **Ryan J. Skarphol** (he/him) is a queer poet from Minneapolis, Minnesota. His poetry has previously appeared in Blue Marble Review, Frost Meadow Review, and The Roaring Muse. He works in Human Services. He is sober.

* **Selene Ceridwen Lee** (she/her) is a Welsh writer with a reverence for free verse and prose poetry that unwinds the equivocal nature of self and sanctity in earth's coils. Instagram @darlinglune

* **Sylvia Marie** (she/her) is a 24-year-old disabled poet who lives in York, UK. She writes for the underdogs and the downtrodden, often covering themes of protest, her queer identity/ trans allyship, equality vs equity, and many more!

✳ **T Cruz** (they/she) is a second-year graduate student at UNCC. They will graduate this May with a master's in English. She is studying the intersectionality of race, religion, and gender, to complete their master's project.

✳ **Tanisha E. Khan** (she/her) is a Canadian writer. She has an MFA in Creative Writing from the University of Oregon, and her work has appeared in "apart, a year of pandemic poetry and prose". When not writing she's on walks, petting local cats and dogs.

✳ **Tommy Cheis** is a Chiricahua writer, diyyin, and Cochise descendant. After traveling extensively through distant lands and meeting interesting people, he resides near the Cochise Stronghold with his horses. His stories (will) appear in Yellow Medicine Review, Rome Review, After Dinner Conversation, NonBinary Review, Ploughshares, Invisible City, University of New Mexico Look to the Mountains Anthology, and many other publications. He is the winner of the Colonel Darren L. Wright Memorial Writing Award, and his work appears in the CLMP Reading List for Native American Heritage Month November 2024. He has been nominated for a PEN Robert J. Dau Short Story Award and a Pushcart Prize. His first novel, RARE EARTH, is on auction; his second, CHILD OF WATER, is on submission.

✳ **Tony Nicholas Clark** (he/him) is a black, trans writer from Pennsylvania. His work has appeared in Short Edition, Soundings East, Perceptions Journal and others. He holds an M.F.A in Creative Writing from Monmouth University.

✳ **Toshiya Kamei** (she/they) is a queer Asian writer who takes inspiration from fairy tales, folklore, and mythology.

www.ingramcontent.com/pod-product-compliance
Lightning Source LLC
Chambersburg PA
CBHW070424310726

48977CB00003B/832